# The Orphan Train to Destiny

❄ ❄ ❄

## Tom Riley

HERITAGE BOOKS
2015

# HERITAGE BOOKS

## AN IMPRINT OF HERITAGE BOOKS, INC.

### Books, CDs, and more—Worldwide

For our listing of thousands of titles see our website
at
www.HeritageBooks.com

Published 2015 by
HERITAGE BOOKS, INC.
Publishing Division
5810 Ruatan Street
Berwyn Heights, Md. 20740

Heritage Books by the author:

*Orphan Train Riders: A Brief History of the Orphan Trail Era (1854–1929)
with Entrance Records from the American Female Guardian
Society's Home for the Friendless in New York
Volume One*

*Orphan Train Riders: Entrance Records from the
American Female Guardian Society's Home
for the Friendless in New York
Volume Two*

*The Orphan Train to Destiny*

International Standard Book Numbers
Paperbound: 978-0-7884-5642-8
Clothbound: 978-0-7884-6149-1

# CHAPTER I

Theodore Roosevelt Sr. was leaving a Republican Party meeting when an emaciated boy covered in sores and vermin tugged at his sleeve and said, "Mister, could you help me. My friend is dying, he can hardly breathe." Roosevelt, a philanthropist and founder of the Children's Aid Society was led to a sewer pipe on Eldridge Street in lower Manhattan. He heard whimpering and coughing from inside the pipe. "I got help, Johnny. This man is gonna get you shelter and a doctor! Come on out, you're gonna be OK." Roosevelt reached into the pipe and slowly coaxed him out. "Easy mister, he's sick bad," said Tom.

The two boys, Tom Gallagher, seven, and John Brady, five, had been sharing the same sewer pipe for the last several days after being chased out of Tully's Bar where they had built a short-lived shoe shining business that the older boys resented. They threatened the two boys and relieved them of their day's earnings and took over their business. After being forced to vacate their prized spot and backroom bed, they began a search for lodging, warmth and food. It was one of the coldest winters the citizens of New York had ever experienced and Tom and John huddled together inside the pipe on frigid nights. Little John's constant coughing and listlessness prompted Tom to seek medical help for his companion. It was the little ones who suffered the most at the hands of adults, gangs and the law of the concrete jungle. New York City in the nineteenth century could be a brutal place for a child abandoned to its mean streets. On any day 12,000-15,000 orphaned and abandoned children could be found wandering the streets in search of food, lodging, clothes and warmth.

John and Tom's parents had both died within twenty-seven days of each other before reaching the Port of New York in Coffin Ships from County Sligo, Ireland. The Coffin Ships were floating warehouses devoid of amenities and used by the people of Ireland for transport during The Great Hunger (1845-1852). Only 60% of the starving and sick passengers who boarded them survived the long trans-Atlantic journey to America. The three mast ships rose above the sea, like crosses on Calvary, carrying the emaciated bodies of children as young as three months to skeletal boys and girls yearning for the cornucopia of America where they would be free of the tyranny of British rule and indifference to their plight.

Mothers and fathers shared their meager possessions with their children, often going without food so their offspring would survive the journey. Bread, fruit, utensils and whatever foodstuff they were allowed to bring aboard was hoarded in burlap sacks and rationed out in the event of a catastrophe at sea, like winter storms, hurricanes and sinking in rough seas. There were rowboats aboard reserved for the captain and his crew (being honorable employees of The Adirondack Timber Company); they had first rights in the event the ship was sinking. They were instructed to take aboard women and children if there was room but not to exceed the maximum safety limitations.

You had about a twenty percent chance of surviving a major storm in a row boat in the Atlantic Ocean, especially those supplied by timber companies who competed with each other to meet the burgeoning demand for lumber and wood products from Canada and America. These bare bones floating storehouses carried their timber loads to Europe and brought back to

America and Canada the wretched and starving refugees of Great Britain's insidious policy of indifference and mean spiritedness instituted by Cabinet Member of the Interior, Charles Trevalyan toward its Irish Colony. It was a policy backed by Queen Victoria and the British Parliament. A policy designed to bring to its knees a nation of subjugated and rebellious people by any means possible. It was a policy to expropriate the fertile fields of Irish landholders and reduce them to tenant farmers.

"The worst thing Great Britain can do is to have the Irish people dependent on Mother England to feed them. We have allotted them their five acre plots and their potatoes to feed their bellies, let us not make them dependent on our largess, lest they become like babies and an eternal drain on our treasury. A policy of benign neglect is the policy I advise our Parliament to pursue, a policy our Queen concurs with," said Charles Trevalyan.

# Chapter II

Andrew Horace Burke was born May 15th, 1850 aboard *The Adirondack Star*, a floating warehouse which delivered oak, white pine, maple, walnut and ash trunks to be milled in London and distributed throughout Europe to meet the insatiable demand of Europe's burgeoning cities for lumber from the New World, their own forests depleted from centuries of use and misuse. Instead of returning to America and Canada empty handed, the ship's owners realized they could make a fortune off The Great Hunger by ferrying victims of The Famine to the New World. They were called Coffin Ships because as many as forty percent of the passengers died en route or soon after reaching America.

Jack and Mary Burke already weakened from long term hunger had managed to make it to the Port of Sligo. Mary's sister, Rita had given them the money for the voyage to America and fed them from her own meager cupboard knowing Mary was already eight months pregnant, in dire condition and running a fever. They boarded *The Star* carrying all their worldly goods in two burlap sacks. Mary carried sixty-four dollars in her purse, money she had put away for a rainy day and a new start in America. Mary was to die of a heart attack hours after Andrew was born. Mary's heart had actually changed shape after years of diminishing nutrition and reduced calorie intake. Mary weighed ninety-one pounds when she died in Jack's arms. She was buried at sea in a short ceremony three days before *The Adirondack Star* steamed into the Port of New York.

4

All European immigrants had to pass through The Saint George Immigration Center on Staten Island; Ellis Island didn't come into being until 1892 in response to the revolutions and wars occurring in Europe. Jack Burke and his newborn son were sent to Marine Hospital where they were fed and clothed and treated for any infection. In the field in back of the hospital trenchs were hastily dug and stacks of bodies of those who didn't survive the trans-Atlantic journey, or who succumbed to the effects of starvation after arrival, found their final resting place. The bodies were covered with lime but the stench of so much death in a confined area made for restive neighbors and occasional riots broke out and not a few of the intake buildings were burned to the ground. Many bodies were later dug up and thrown into the harbor to make room for new deceased arrivals.

New York City in the nineteenth century could be a brutal place for a child. A magnet to immigrants and the poor in search of a job, the city was also a haven for gamblers, thieves and murderers. When adults fell victim to alcoholism, prostitution or drug addiction, their children were the first to suffer. Jack Burke and his one year old son, Andrew found a tavern, The Five Points on Canal Street in lower Manhattan, that rented out space in a back room for two dollars a month. Forty two people were housed in the room which contained a separate entrance in the back. There was a cacophony of languages spoken with those of the same ethnic group keeping together. Not a few of the tenants were unwed mothers and battered women with children. It was a refuge from the freezing cold weather and food could be ordered from the tavern. There was one running faucet and several people gave themselves sponge baths. Buckets were set up in the alley for people to relieve themselves. Every morning a cart came by and picked them up, replaced them with empty buckets and dumped the feces, vomit and urine off the pier into the Hudson River.

Jack reclined in a corner and held his son in his lap. He missed Molly terribly and wondered how he could care for Andy and get work to feed and house them. He was down to his last twelve dollars. He missed his farm, his children and the good life that had been his just three years ago. Molly and he had been the proud owners of a 300 acre farm in County Sligo that produced an abundant crop of soy beans, peas, wheat, tomatoes, apples, potatoes, rye and hops. Housed in their barn were four Arabian steeds purchased at a bargain price from an Arab sheik who had asked Burke to train his stable because of his renown in racing circles for building bloodlines by doing genealogical research. Burke built his reputation on an innate fondness for horses and years of experience in training them. When the Sligo Library was about to close because of a lack of funds Burke stepped in and paid the required amount of rent to the Crown. Being an avid reader he came across a volume on genealogy and felt it applied to all of God's creatures. He began applying genealogical research to horse races in Dublin and Belfast and betting small amounts on the results.

He soon gained a reputation in tracing the genealogy of winning horses and picking little known steeds that dominated the European racing season. The sheik's appreciation of his intellectual powers and training methods allowed Jack to expand his farm into the paradise on earth it was to the twelve Burke children: Charles, Donald, Thomas, David, Daniel, Rita, Robert, John, Elizabeth, Dorothy, William and Andrew. Jack and Mary Burke were only a handful of Catholic landowners who had managed to accrue a substantial estate in spite of laws preventing Catholics from owning more than five acres. Lord Ashburton had granted a dispensation to the

Burkes because of Jack's management and acumen in breeding and training horses that were dominating the London racing circuit.

Charles, Donald and Thomas finished the seeding of fifty acres of potato seedlings imported from Maine. Their father had traveled to Belfast to retrieve the seedlings which were advertised in agricultural journals as producing super potatoes, the likes of which had never been seen before in Europe. Little did the Burke children know that lurking in these "super potatoes" from Maine was the airborne fungus, Phytophthora infestans, a particularly herculean fungus that would reduce the population of Ireland from eight million people to five million; 1.2 million would die of starvation and another two million souls would leave Ireland for America, Canada, Australia, England and Scotland. It would create a hell on earth for the Burke family.

The Burke girls would be shipped off to Australia to be future brides to a continent bereft of women. The boys sought work wherever they could find it, but failing that some went to London, Glasgow and Canada. Lord Ashburton renounced his contract to Jack Burke forcing him into tenant farming of just five acres of the virus infected potato plot. When Burke protested the seizure of his farm, a band of hired thugs broke into his farmhouse, ransacked the home and threatened violence to the family. The thugs found the contract, tore it up in front of the children and threw it into the peat fireplace.

The family's potato crop would turn into a black gooey mess and within two years Lord Ashburton, a London financier and absentee landlord, would own Jack and Molly's 300 acre farm. Cromwell's invasion of Ireland and his intense hatred of Roman Catholicism barred Irish Catholics from owning more than five acres of land. He exported Irish children to the West Indies so they could work the sugar plantations. Lord Robert Peel attempted to alleviate the famine by exporting 100,000 tons of corn to a country he never visited and which had no mills to grind it; thereby causing untold stomach disorders among a starving people. The corn was to be known as Peel's Brimstone. Britain's policy of neglect, indifference and eviction meant London's grip on power in Ireland was reaching its zenith.

Jack's reveries were broken by the sound of a marching band on Canal Street. With Andy in his arms he went out in the cold air where he confronted a crowd gathering around a group of women baring a banner declaring The American Female Guardian Society for Moral Reform. It was a temperance organization which had started twenty years earlier when a group of women were outraged at the fact that young girls were resorting to prostitution because of poverty and abandonment. They railed against the evils of alcohol and implored the citizens of the Five Points area to refrain from alcohol, gambling and drugs.

"Residents of the Five Points Tavern, we've established a Home for the Friendless at 22 Warren Street. Leave this den of inequity and alcoholic stupor and renounce the purveyors of poison that live off your honest wages. Come to our new home and sign a pledge to refrain from alcohol and the debris it leaves behind: broken families, abandoned children, malnourishment, and disease. Come and accept the Lord and be changed. The American Female Guardian Society has purchased an abandoned brewery on Warren Street and have turned it into a Temple of the Lord to those who want a better life. We have clean sleeping quarters, a dining room, a clinic, a chapel and a school for children if you fathers and mothers renounce your former ways and seek the Lord where he may be found.," said a commanding young lady to the gathering crowd.

Several young toughs under the direction of the tavern owner exited the front door and began to taunt the young lady. "Go back to yer church, yer Holy Rollers and let us drink in peace. These people know what's best for them, so get out of here!" Suddenly a few bottles rained through the air and smashed against the dung covered cobblestones narrowly missing the speaker. The ladies rapidly gathered their banners and the crowd dispersed in all direction. The AFGS women regrouped and the marching band picked up its tempo and continued down Canal Street. Jack and young Andy followed the group for several hours and a beacon of hope built to a crescendo when Jack entered the refurbished brewery The American Female Guardian Society had built. At a time when there was no social safety net, these intrepid women, all volunteers, offered a home, food, shelter and more to the homeless, infirm, alcoholics and children. They were America's first social workers. They kept records and sent out newsletters to every protestant church across America detailing the squalor and the dire condition of children in America's largest city. Jack saw the opportunity it offered to care for Andrew while he sought work. He signed on, agreed to their by-laws and both he and Andy were treated to a hot meal and housed in a small room. Jack felt tremendous gratitude for these selfless women and their mission. He promised that once he found work he would repay them.

# Chapter III

After two years and six months at the AFGS facility Jack and Andy thrived. Although a nominal Catholic, Jack was grateful for the hospitality this Protestant organization had provided. It literally saved their lives, Andy was growing into a robust and lively three-year-old and Jack had a job in a shoe factory. He gave the AFGS money to care for his son while he was at work. In three years Jack worked his way up to supervisor of the sole cutting floor which employed eight men and three women. He was gone twelve hours a day, six days a week; all the time saving money to buy a house, something he had promised Mary he would do in the New World. He had even met a co-worker who knew Mary's sister, Rita and a relationship was blossoming.

Tragedy struck on June 9th, 1854 when an explosion in the tannery on a lower floor resulted in a fire that incinerated the men and women above them. The owner of the shoe factory had locked all doors leading to safety, only to be opened at the end of the shift when the employees could go home. Jack's incinerated body was found with the others at the exit door. They had managed to pull the door off its hinges but were overcome by smoke. The owner paid for the skeletal remains to be buried in Potter's Field. Forty-eight workers died in the fire and many workers were crippled for life, jumping from windows. Jack's savings were to lie unclaimed. The AFGS was notified of Andy's father's death and, at the age of four, Andy was sent to the Children's Aid Society on West 23rd Street. The Children's Aid Society had just been established a year earlier by Charles Loring Brace, Theodore Roosevelt Sr.

and a group of like-minded philanthropists appalled at the sight of 10,000-15,000 orphans wandering the streets of New York, walking around with open sores and living in sewer pipes and alleyways.

For five years Andrew Burke lived in a dormitory with twenty-four other boys hawking newspapers in the newspaper wars of the era. He was obligated to pay twelve cents a day for sleeping quarters and three meals a day at the Newsboy's Lodge on 14th Street. It was July 1859 when he and other boys were summoned to 23$^{rd}$ Street for an announcement by Charles Loring Brace. As the boys entered the auditorium and took their seats, Brace took center stage and asked for quiet. "Tomorrow children, you will begin a journey to a new life. Christian families across America are awaiting your arrival. Many of you are already spoken for and your new guardians are awaiting your arrival. Others will be chosen at the Town Hall or center of village life; still others of you will be picked at the railroad platform in small towns. Be on your best behavior, those of you who have not been chosen will return by train to The Children's Aid Society for placement at another time. Make sure you bring your Bibles with you. You will be given a small packing case. Please destroy any letters or contact information you may have of relatives and friends here in the city. You are moving on to a better life in the American countryside. You know work; your bodies have been strengthened for the journey; your open sores and ailments healed. Now you will experience family life and you'll be treated like a son or daughter, as many of your sisters will be traveling with you. We will be leaving from Grand Central Terminal; our train departs at 9 am. I want you all to meet here at 7 am for our walk to Grand Central. Make the best of it; may God bless you all." said Mr. Brace.

The children filed from the Assembly Hall and went to their dormitories. This was to be their last day at the Newsboy's Lodging House. For the last three years Andrew Burke had earned his keep selling newspapers. Now a whole new chapter was opening up for him. He was glad to be ending his career hawking newspapers and glad that his friends were going with him out west. There was anxiety too, as he knew several boys who hadn't been picked by foster parents. They had been returned to New York and told stories of having been treated like cattle, manhandled by farmers feeling their muscles and sizing them up as farmhands. Some of the farmers stuck their fingers into the children's mouths not wanting to have to pay for dental work. Still others seemed genuinely interested in the children and wanted to give them a better life. He went to bed that night tossing and turning, wondering what the future held for him.

As the train left Grand Central Station with forty-five boys and girls, Andrew found himself sitting next to an older boy, John. They shared stories about their life as newsboys and The Children's Aid Society and came to the realization they both had come to America on Coffin ships from Ireland. Both of John's parents had expired on the journey and he'd been found living in a sewer pipe by Theodore Roosevelt Sr., one of the founders of the Children's Aid Society. "The man saved my life and I'll never forget him." Andrew shared his experience with his father and how he'd been saved by The American Female Guardian Society. As the train rolled into Indiana with half the boys and girls still waiting to be taken in by foster parents, the boys had developed a friendship that unknowingly would last a lifetime. When they reached Noblesville, Indiana they were taken to the Town Hall. Judge Harold Green looked over the boys and girls, decided that this New York tough, John was to his liking, "I wonder what I can make of this kid."

A farmer and his wife picked Andrew Burke. As they were chosen and taken to a table where foster parents signed papers and promised to raise the children as their own, they whispered to each other to keep in touch. John and Andrew looked back at the stage where other children were being looked over by the excited crowd and wondered what awaited them.

After three years on the farm Andrew Burke left the horses in the field and went off to join the Civil War. He was twelve years old and General Latimer was looking for a drummer boy. He was tired of working seven days a week and had heard of the formation of the 75thBrigade. He walked eight miles to town and was accepted by the General himself. For the next two years he was to see tremendous carnage and was relieved of his position when General Latimer was wounded and gave Andrew his discharge.

Andrew went to work as a cashier in a general store. The Civil War had turned him into a serious young man and he decided he needed to further his education. He attended Asbury College for two years and found he had a good mind for math. He was elected county treasurer and served in that position for six years. He joined the Masons and steadily rose in the ranks of that organization. He moved with his new wife to the Dakota Territories and was elected treasurer of Cass County and later nominated as governor of North Dakota.

# Chapter IV

A lone eagle broke through the morning mist, soared along the rocky, pebble-strewn beach and glided to a perch atop a scraggly pine jutting at an angle from the cliffs of Haley's Point in Juneau, Alaska. John Green turned in his saddle and followed the flight of the eagle when he broke from his perch as the sound of human voices pierced the early morning mist. The eagle released the clam shell in his claws into the windswept waves crashing against the coast. John peered down the beveled hills to his right to the speckled forest below. He saw motion between the pines and three men on horseback could be seen meandering up the winding trail that led to Haley's Point. He hadn't had company in three days and if he was to do the Lord's work and preach the Gospel it meant dealing with the prospectors, miners, railroad workers, Indians and plain folk who inhabited this part of Alaska. He wanted to avoid the bandits, roving gangs of disgruntled riffraff who created havoc and the occasional psychotic loner roaming about looking for easy prey.

John Green Brady had plans for Alaska and no man was better suited to make them come true. A graduate of Yale University's Divinity School with a minor in business, he had come to Alaska as a missionary, to convert the heathen masses and give them a vision of the golden opportunities that awaited them if they aligned themselves to Christ. Alaska might be a territory of America but it was his dream to unite the opposing forces of this bountiful land by means of the railroad, business opportunities and its abundance of natural resources. He felt it was his calling to lead Alaska into the twentieth century and toward its ultimate goal, statehood. But first things first, he needed votes to accomplish his goal of becoming mayor of Juneau. Statehood could wait. He watched as the horsemen slowly maneuvered their mounts along the boulder strewn trail. The sure-footedness of horses hoisting 1,500 pounds plus rider up steep inclines constantly amazed him.

"Hi there, gentlemen, it so good to have company, mind if I tag along? I'm just returning from Sitka, where are you guys headed?" The three bearded men, in various states of disarray, eyed him with suspicion. One man had his hand on the butt of a rifle holstered in a scabbard. Seeing antagonism in his bloodshot eyes, and annoyance in his traveling companions, John resorted to a disarming question. "I'll leave you gentlemen alone, if you wish, I'm traveling to Juneau to minister to my flock," he said, pulling a Bible from his saddlebag. When he looked up all three men had pulled out their pistols and slowly cocked them, aiming at his midsection.

"No need for violence, gentlemen. Calm down, it's no way to treat a Samaritan traveling to do the Lord's work," said John. Two of the men sheepishly holstered their guns while the third did not. "Get in front of us, so we can keep an eye on you." John did as he was told and led them on a long journey into Juneau, all the while regaling them with Biblical stories, the need for repentance, forgiveness and salvation. With each mile their hostility lessened and by the time they got to Juneau they parted amicably with the men promising to pay a visit to his church. One of the men asked for a special blessing to be reunited with his wife and child, whom he had abandoned under the influence of too much drink.

John entered the Juneau Presbyterian Church and glanced at the church bulletin board and saw a large poster supporting his candidacy for mayor. He knew the debate held at the courthouse could devolve into violence if Soapy Smith chose actual intimidation against him and the town's people. His men might be present in force but John knew Soapy looked forward to debating him, having already intimidated half the town and now seeking to bring around the rest. John Green knew the issues and was confident he could make his case as usual even against formidable odds. He settled into his desk chair and quietly reflected on his life before nodding off from twelve hours in the saddle.

# Chapter V

John pushed the swinging doors and entered the Water Inn Hole Saloon. Sue Brown, the proprietor, eyed the handsome Irishman as he chose a table facing the piano man. She walked up behind him and stood with her arms folded. Several couples near the piano melted away when they saw the angry expression on her face. When Sue Brown was mad, the object of her wrath had nowhere to hide in Juneau, for it was rumored she was worth $20 million dollars and that some men would kill for her at the drop of a hat.

"Susan Brown, what can I do for you?" asked John as he savored the fragrance of the finest French perfume money could buy. John often came to the Water Inn Hole just to smell her choice of perfume for the day as she held court over the assorted con artists, murderers, businessmen, honest prospectors and millionaire claim jumpers who frequented the tastefully decorated saloon, inn and house of ill repute. He knew half the men in Juneau were secretly in love with Sue. Prospecting a claim and protecting it from claim jumpers kept men from civilization and the joys that could be found in Juneau's pleasure palace, the Water Inn Hole. It was the citadel of gambling, drink, news from around the world, especially America and pleasures of the flesh.

"I hear you refuse to sell Brady's Bonanza to my attorney. You know it's a worthless claim. You've been here two years now hovering over twelve acres of nothingness and giving it that silly name Brady's Bonanza! It is laughable, that you would hold out from my offer of $50,000, knowing I own all the claims surrounding it. You are a Luddite, John Green Brady, hindering progress and refusing to see the inevitable come to fruition. The dredges are all warehoused. Time is money Reverend Brady and I won't stand for your recalcitrance much longer," said Sue, in a smoky, velvet voice.

"That's right, Sue," said John as he quietly pushed the chair opposite him with his foot to allow her a seat. Sue brushed past him and slid into the chair, her kelly green silk dress highlighted her stunning figure. In the background near the bar, one of her hired guns positioned himself for a clean shot at the Reverend if given the order. John took in Sue's aura and realized why men melted in her presence and sold their claims to her taking the $50,000 offer and ridding themselves of their mosquito ridden claims and heading south where the winters were warmer and female companionship more plentiful. They also wanted to increase their longevity and escape the law of the jungle that persisted especially with Soapy Smith and his roving gang of misfits taking over claims through violence and intimidation. John inhaled the fragrance of the perfume and gathered his thoughts. It was so rare in Alaska to be in the presence of a beautiful woman, a natural beauty with blonde hair worn in a variety of styles, sensuous lips and brown eyes that sparkled with ire, disapproval, laughter or warmth depending on the occasion.

Sue was attracted to his manly stature and his flowing black hair that splayed over broad shoulders that hinted at a well-muscled body due to years of hard labor at the Green Farm in Indiana. Years at Yale majoring in theology, business and physical education had sharpened his physique and made him attractive to women. His face possessed a fashionable mustache and sky blue eyes that were joyful and alive as if each day was a gift. His countenance always seemed to possess a wisdom that set him free of anxieties that beset most men.

"It's the only claim I own, Sue. I've been working on it as long as I can remember. I love the property, the fishing is good, the salmon plentiful. It has hills and meadows and trees galore and I built the cabin with my own two hands. I love this land, why should I sell it it? I also like the fact it is near Juneau, my church and my congregation. And the variety of trees I have on my property gives me great pleasure," said John. "Besides, I'm opposed to you scarring the land with your mechanical dredges. You're killing off the salmon run and muddying a pristine river and that racket your dredges make keeps me awake at night."

"Trees, salmon, pristine rivers, give me a break, the only thing that matters is the yellow gold in them thar hills. Accept my offer and you can live a life of luxury. Refuse it and you incur my wrath and that of Soapy Smith, who'll do anything to become the mayor of Juneau. Aren't you afraid of what's going to happen if you keep going up against him? People don't wind up well when they oppose Soapy." said Sue.

"If we are ever going to achieve statehood, we need more than an economy based on gold prospecting which scars the land. Alaska is filled with natural resources, timber, fresh water, wild life and natural beauty. If we're to attract people, there's a need for law abiding citizens and middle class people who want to establish businesses and grow families. Soapy and his men threaten public harmony. If he were to become mayor, then the inmates have taken over Juneau and all of us will have to deal with daily extortion, lawlessness and expropriation of property, including you, Sue. Everything you own will fall into his hands. Side with what is right and back my candidacy and Juneau will prosper and grow under the rule of law," said John, more determined than ever to end the scourge of lawlessness caused by Soapy and his gang.

"You also have no right to despoil the river. You are driving a stake through the heart of every man who makes a living on the river and depends on it for salmon and other fish. In less than a year we'll never see the salmon again. The silt washing down the river will destroy their habitat and wash away their eggs," said John warming to the argument. He could see Sue's face flushing with anger. He wanted to hit harder. "And what are you using to extract the gold from the placer? I bet you are using mercury right there on the barge site." Sue started breathing rapidly. John slammed his hand on the table. "I knew I was right! You idiot," he said pointing directly at Sue. Her face reddened with fury, but John wasn't finished. He wanted to kill the project in its infancy. "Don't you realize what will happen? Haven't those geology people from San Francisco you hired told you the consequences of releasing mercury into the river? All known life along the Cripple River will die. The stuff will settle on the bottom and be ingested by fish. They will die almost immediately and the river will be polluted for centuries."

"You pompous, phony pseudo-intellectual, what have you done for Juneau and what gives you the right to attack me? If we depended on the likes of you there would be no Juneau. Juneau was created out of self-interest; men who saw a profit and went after it. Banks, hotels, saloons and general stores are created because they are needed. For your information I built the only school house in Juneau. What you said about mercury, I'll clear with my geologist. I provide 200 families with wages from my businesses. How many do you take care of, preacher?"

# Chapter VI

As a drummer boy for the 75th Regiment Andrew Horace Burke had seen the horrors of war and had known bone chilling fear. His youthful enthusiasm for battle had completely disappeared and after the Battle of Bull Run he abandoned the Regiment and returned to Indiana with the understanding from the Colonel he would continue his education, thanks to Lincoln's benefits to veterans. The war had changed him and left him with revulsion at the loss of life he had seen all around him and the necessity to achieve and utilize all one's talent to benefit mankind. He married his childhood sweetheart, Caroline Cleveland and worked the register at a general store. He attended Asbury College and found he had an aptitude for math. He spent a year there developing his mind and trying to forget the horrors of the Civil War. He was asked to become county treasurer and continued his interest in politics.

In 1880 he and his wife arrived in Casselton, North Dakota with only sixty-five dollars. He worked as a bookkeeper before becoming a cashier with the First National Bank of Casselton. He entered public service as the treasurer of Cass County, a position he held for six years. On November 4th, 1890 he was elected governor by popular vote. During Burke's administration, it was discovered that North Dakota did not have laws for the selection of presidential electors, and he called a special session to ensure that the state could participate in the 1892 elections. Burke lost favor with farmers when he vetoed a bill which would have forced railroads to lease sites near the tracks for building grain elevators and warehouses under conditions that were not acceptable to the railroads. During his term The Normal School of Valley City and Mayville were established and Fargo became the site of the state's Agricultural College (Now North Dakota State University). State bonds were secured to pay the Dakota Territory deficit, and a commission was formed to frame state laws. After running unsuccessfully for reelection, Burke returned to private life. He later served as an inspector with the U.S. land Office in Washington, D.C.

# Chapter VII

Brady left the Water Inn Hole and walked down the wooden sidewalk pondering his conversation with Sue Brown. Juneau was bustling with activity. The prospectors were coming out of the hills to stock up on supplies to carry them over the coming winter. News of newly discovered mother lodes was coming out of the hills daily. Dirt poor plough boys and farmers who had left their land to strike it rich were becoming millionaires overnight. Many of the prospectors were short of cash and were working in the saw mills just to pay for supplies to work their claims. Juneau now had a population of over 10,000 and ninety percent were Americans. To John, Americans were a hard drinking, hardworking people with a direct and friendly manner.

He looked across the street where once a large muddy expanse was now giving way to a new block of wooden store fronts. Vanderbilt lumber was the major supplier of fresh cut timber. Jim Vanderbilt had come from New York to strike it rich. While other prospectors were buying up all the claims along the river, Jim was purchasing acres of cedar and evergreens way back in the hills. The prospectors laughed and congratulated themselves about obtaining their riverfront claims and saw nothing but folly in Vanderbilt's purchase of timberland. Jim built the lumber business from scratch and was the largest employer in Juneau and had recently gotten huge orders from Europe to supply timber for its burgeoning cities. His mill was in operation twenty-four hours around the clock. Many prospectors gave up their get rich quick schemes to work for Jim and the steady wages he provided.

The underside to all this expansion was the increase in homelessness, alcoholism, suicides, broken families and orphaned children. John knew of men who slept in crates and heated themselves with a single kerosene lamp. They were often alcoholics, who went bust and lost their claim or had sold them over a card game. Spurred on back East by tabloids publishing tales of unbelievable wealth to be had in Alaska, prospectors came in droves, ill-prepared for the harsh weather and difficult terrain. Many gave up after a few months and the onset of winter, selling their equipment ten cents on the dollar.

After walking eight blocks John came to U-Me's Japanese Restaurant. Johnny had known Margie U-Pak since he came to Alaska. She had worked in the saloons and eateries in Juneau until she saved enough money to open her own restaurant. By that time she was so well known and liked that her place became an immediate success, especially for seafood lovers and those who had acquired a taste for great sushi. "Johnny, where have you been? I haven't seen you since last year's Juneau's dog race: said Margie as she walked up to him and embraced him. "What's this," she said as she plucked a grey hair from his temple. "When are you gonna marry me and settle down. What's your plan for the race this year?"

"I don't know, I been busy with the mayoral election coming up so I was thinking of passing it up this year. My dog, Lancer and I are getting old and I'd have to borrow some dogs. Clem sold his claim and his dogs to Miss Brown," said John.

"You know Sue Brown is offering a $100,000 to the winner of this year's race to Pine Log. It's only August and already twenty-nine teams are entered. Sit with me here, Johnny and fill out one of these forms while I get some coffee for you. Are you hungry? I got some terriyaki and sushi on the grill" said Margie motioning to a tall man in a white chef's hat.

"Hold on, Margie, I just stopped by to say hello. I'll take the coffee. What's this about Miss Brown raising the ante on the race to Pine Log?"

"Al Steinberg is not racing this year. He sold his kennel and is moving to Florida. His wife caught pneumonia last year training his mush team so he doesn't want to take a chance. He sold all his best dogs to Miss Brown so it's going to be hard for anyone to beat her this year. Since Al is leaving she'll be heading The Juneau Days Race Committee. You want cream and sugar? How about a little nip of sake to keep the blood circulating? Johnny, you're getting so thin. Why don't you move in with me and fatten up? We could open up a saloon next door. I was tired of paying rent so I bought Mr. Nagle out. He was glad to sell, his wife died last year so he's moving back to Maryland," said Margie.

"So Miss Brown thinks she has the race all sewed up, does she? She wouldn't be betting $100,000 plus entry fees unless she thinks she's got a sure thing. You racing this year, Margie?" asked Johnny.

"Not this year, Johnny. I almost froze to death last year when that ice hit us on the third day. Ricky and I went twenty miles out of our way after someone moved the markers on the course. At first I thought it was Al Steinberg but then they caught the McCreedy brothers with a marker in their sled when the teams were breaking trails for each other during the ice storm. They've been banned for life, but the rumor is they are sponsoring Soapy Smith and his gang with supplies and dogs."

"They let that low down thief into the race? Why he's the biggest crook in Alaska and he's also running for mayor. He should have been jailed a long time ago but no one wants to take him on.

"There's a rumor that those twenty-one prospectors killed in the Yukon were done in by Soapy and his gang. Seems the law never finds him with his hands dirty. Soapy had always confined his misbehaving to the Yukon but the heat is on up North so he follows the gold down south. Now he's working with the McCreedy brothers and that is trouble with a capital T. Margie, I'll fill this form out for the race if you'll join forces with me. I'll need a team with at least six to eight good mush dogs and supplies buried every fifty miles for the team. The exact location I'll tell you as we get closer to the race. If you get the dogs out to my place by next week we'll start training right away. It's a long shot, but with the ante up like it is even third place will payoff well. I got added incentive to win this race so I'll be going for the gold. What do you say, Margie? I'll put up the entry fee and we split any winnings fifty, fifty," said Johnny.

"Johnny, I love you!" She planted a kiss on his cheek. With you in the race driving the team and Dragon, my best dog, leading the way, we could do it." The tall Japanese chef placed a dish of sushi on a reed mat. A beautiful Japanese woman dressed in a black and red kimono with a large golden fan embroidered on it poured hot Sake into two small glasses. They lifted a toast to their new partnership.

"Fifty, fifty," said Johnny, touching his glass to hers.

"Fifty, fifty," said Margie, her eyes beaming with laughter and delight in anticipation of the stimulating adventure ahead of both of them.

# Chapter VIII

J uneau Dog Days was a celebration in honor of the dogs and sled teams who delivered serum to combat Diphtheria during an outbreak of the disease. One hundred dogs working in relays delivered the needed serum in eight days over 986 miles of blizzards, whiteouts and unbelievable terrain. It was an annual week of feasting, games, pageantry, theater and dog sled racing. The highlight of the day was the start of the dog sled race to Pine Log. This 375 mile trek pitted the best drivers and the best mush team against each other for the honor of receiving $20,000 in prize money. Miss Brown, in an attempt to boost her popularity and the acceptance of her dredging company on the Cripple River, had raised the ante an additional $100,000 bringing the total to $120,000. The first team to reach the halfway point was to receive $25,000. The eventual winners received $50,000, $25,000 and $20,000, respectively.

John's best finish was third place in last year's race. He completed the course in five days and ten hours. The course ran through some of the most difficult terrain to be found in Alaska. John had narrowly escaped an avalanche that buried two of his dogs. He was in the process of tethering two new lead dogs when he looked up and saw half the mountainside break off. Jumping on his sled he forced his team just out of the reach of a 100 foot wall of snow and ice. The untethered lead dogs ran off in the opposite direction and were buried alive. Five teams passed him within hours because of the lost lead dogs. His exhausted team managed to pass one of the teams when it followed a misplaced marker and went twenty miles in the wrong direction. The McCreedy brothers, who had finished fourth, were later disqualified when Al Steinberg and several others told of finding a marker in their sled while breaking trail. Breaking trail was a period of cooperation in the race when heavily drifted snow made the trail impassible for anyone's team. The teams would gather at this point and agree to take the lead at different intervals so as not to completely tire out one team. During this period they would exchange information, buy or bargain off dogs and share warm drinks and supplies. If a severe snow storm covered the markers, the teams would gather and pitch tents and spend the night drinking, making tea and singing songs about Alaska. If someone was injured or needed medical attention and agreed to turn back for the injured party, the judges would award that team $5,000.

Once the trail was cleared it was every man and woman for themselves. Teams would pass each other without a word. This was to be the fifth year the race to Pine Log was held. The dastardly deeds of the McCreedy brothers had cast a pall over the race, but more entrants than ever agreed to sign up because of Sue Brown's largesse increasing the ante. There were calls in *The Juneau Daily* for calling off the race, because it was beginning to attract unsavory characters like Soapy Smith and his gang. Miss Brown, in an attempt to keep the race honest, had asked the Juneau police force to monitor the race.

John received Dragon and eight Alaskan huskies from Margie. He went into the hills and got six of his own dogs from Nahari Kennels. He had put them there for breeding purposes every year after the racing season was over. When Dragon saw the old team he immediately established dominance over them by bowling over the young males and giving them a well-placed nip. Sweetpea, Johnny's favorite dog and Dragon were wary of each other and occasionally menaced each other with fierce growls. John realized they couldn't work together and would have to replace each other at the lead. Within a few days, the remainder of the dogs had chosen sides and two mush teams were developed.

John began training them by having each dog pull a wheeled cart loaded with rocks. Slowly he began to increase the weight and duration of the run so the dogs could develop stamina. Then he began to put combinations of dogs together to see how they cooperated with each other while increasing the rock load in the cart. Sometimes he worked them well past midnight. He also began work on the two sleds he would need for mountainous terrain, heavily wooded areas and frozen lakes. One of the sleds would be his speed sled for the dash across the tundra into Pine Log. His friend, Huang had given him bamboo; it had been bought in Seattle and was stored in his house.

There was a knock at his door. John opened it to see the smiling face of Chuck Harris. "Had to shoe a couple of mules for your pretty neighbor upstream, said Chuck. Paid me well to leave my shop and do the job on site," said Chuck as he shook Johnny's hand with his huge callused paw. "The dredging begins in a couple of weeks. It's going to revolutionize things around here. I think we're in a new era, Johnny. The future of gold mining belongs to the big companies now. The dredge alone is said to extract more gold from the Cripple River than 5,000 prospectors working their claims for a year."

"Tell me Chuck, that you're not affected by what's happening to our forest and rivers. Now you can see whole mountains stripped of trees to supply lumber for Juneau whose population has grown ten times what it was two years ago. Those recent rains washed away several houses in a mudslide. And don't get me started

29

on the fish kills we're starting to experience. The mercury the miners are using to extract gold from placer is definitely why the river is getting smelly. When dredging starts you can say goodbye to the salmon in a year or two. The silt will destroy the eggs after a while." said John.

"Well, John, the business community is behind you in your run for mayor. Homelessness is becoming a big problem, with men living in tool crates. They lost their stake in a card game or ran out of money or just plain luck. We ain't got enough doctors, venereal disease is spreading among the whores and kids are dying because they don't have shelter. If we don't get somebody elected who knows the place, then the company stooges will run the city, get their own men elected and they'll rubber stamp whatever the company wants," said Chuck.

"Soapy Smith is coming into town tomorrow to debate me. See if you can fill the hall with my supporters. I know he'll be bringing his own entourage, so I'll need the support," said John.

# Chapter IX

Andrew Horace Burke ran through a volley of gun fire to reach Corporal Thompson when he saw the man drop like a rock after he had taken a bullet through the chest. Upon reaching him he tried to stanch the flow of blood by applying pressure with his hands but the gushing continued. "I don't want to die, my wife and kids need me at the farm," whispered Thompson.

It was 1863 and chaos reigned all around them in the battle for Gettysburg. Andy was only fourteen and he looked at his bloody hands and was sick and tired of losing so many friends. The older men had borne the brunt of the struggle over the last two years of the war. "Help me, I'm dying:' whimpered Thompson. Andy felt his pulse weakening as he tried to bandage the wound. Blood was everywhere and drenched Andy's uniform. The fusillade of gun fire picked up and he knew the Union was losing many soldiers. "Why did I run way from the farm? I got caught up in the glory of patriotism and war but this is the reality and it makes no sense, so many young men cut down in their prime," he said, thinking. "You're going to be OK, Thompson, just hang in there. We'll get you to a field hospital soon." said Andy, knowing Thompson had lost too much blood. The young man drew his last breath and expired. Andy knew what he had to do as he ran forward to aid another fallen soldier.

Burke went to visit Brigade Commander General Latimer who was recovering from wounds at the Battle of Gettysburg. After a few pleasantries about the

Commander's health, Burke nervously made his request. "I've spent the last two years serving under you, General and Gettysburg has done me in. I lost so many of my friends. I'm asking to be relieved as drummer boy and medic and want to return home to Indiana. I'm depressed, tired and emotionally drained and feel I can't perform as a soldier any more. I'm asking you to sign my separation papers as I was under age when I joined and have performed to the best of my ability."

General Latimer said, "Andy, I couldn't ask you to do more; you insisted in joining our brigade at the tender age of twelve, I tried to dissuade you, you performed admirably but this war gets to everybody. I'm agreeing to your request and will give you an honorable discharge which will make you eligible for benefits President Lincoln just put in effect. You've done your duty. I wish you the best of fortune in whatever you choose to do." Andrew Horace Burke left the hospital elated that his request had been granted. The horrors of war were behind him but the memories would linger forever.

For several years he worked in a grocery store and attended Ashbury College under the G.I. Bill. He excelled at math and took courses in accounting and philosophy. A year shy of receiving his degree he began experiencing night sweats, headaches and nightmares. He was suffering from post-traumatic stress and had to drop out of college. He continued to work in the grocery store until his application for a job in the local bank was accepted. He rapidly advanced in the bank to head teller. After marrying Caroline Cleveland, he moved to Casselton, North Dakota, and became a general store bookkeeper.

He next became a cashier of The First National Bank of Casselton and then, for six years, the treasurer of Cass County. Burke was elected to the governorship in 1890 as a Republican. During Burke's administration it was discovered that North Dakota did not have any laws for the selection of presidential electors. Burke called for a special session of the legislature to convene on June 1, 1891, and attended to the law. The state participated in the 1892 U.S. presidential election when Grover Cleveland was elected to a second term as president of the United States. The Republican elector voted for Benjamin Harrison, while the other two electors split, one voting for Cleveland and the other for Weaver.

Burke's political career ended when he lost favor with farmers of the state by vetoing a bill that would have forced the railroads to lease sites near the tracks for building grain elevators and warehouses under conditions that were not acceptable to the railroads. After unsuccessfully running for re-election he retired to private life and later was an inspector with the U.S. Land Office in Washington, D.C. Governor Andrew Horace Burke passed away in Roswell, New Mexico, in 1918.

# Chapter X

Mayor Biggs, the outgoing mayor of Juneau dismissed the three party hacks he had designated mayoral candidates when Soapy Smith handed him $50,000 to nominate him as the party's candidate. He had hoped more reputable concerns would have come forward with major contributions, but $50,000 was not to be dismissed lightly.

On a personal level Mayor Biggs disliked Soapy Smith immensely. He was a foul mouthed, vile smelling, violent man who reeked of whiskey. The fact that he shot a bullet into the ceiling while Biggs was outlining his accomplishments had caused great anxiety among the audience gathered for the debate. "Mayor Biggs, you can dispense with the flowery oratory because I'll be dictating what my campaign plans are for Juneau. As soon as I'm elected to office I plan to tax everyone holding a claim within a thirty mile radius of Juneau. They'll be paying a City Prospector's Fee of ten percent on all their earnings. This will be used to pay for roads and sewerage into the mountains and far flung hamlets of our great city. Right boys!" said Soapy, turning to his grimy entourage of supporters monopolizing the front seats.

"We're with you, Soapy," they cried out in unison. A few of the more rambunctious supporters raised their guns and were about to fire into the ceiling, when Soapy cast a baleful glance their way.

"I'll be leading the parade here, gentlemen," he shouted as he drew his Colt .45. "From now on you smelly, whiskey laden criminals will clean up your act or else! The citizens of Juneau will demand no less!" said Soapy as he pointed his gun at the audience and waved it across the assemblage. I demand absolute adherence to my campaign plans. The collection of taxes will begin on the 2nd of January. We want the citizens of Juneau to have a Happy New Year. The Prospector's Fee along with license fees for all businesses plus a liquor tax will be due by the end of January. Those failing to pay these fees and taxes by April 15th will be sentenced to thirty days in jail by Judge Kerr. We will begin construction on a road network into the far flung hamlets that will be halted because of lack of funds; we will raise taxes...."

The speech when on for more than forty-five minutes with a total of eighty-five new taxes and fees mentioned. There was a subtle ominous threat to create havoc in Juneau should he lose the election. Soapy and his entourage left the building before John Green Brady mounted the stage to give his speech. He sensed an element of fear and disaster lurking in the people's hearts as they envisioned a future should Soapy Smith be elected Mayor.

"I know most of you pretty well. You know Juneau is capable of a better future. Evil will not triumph here. It has raised its head and threatened the body, which is the people. I believe in people and your belief in what we can accomplish brings us all here today. If you elect me mayor we are going to have a peaceful city. We are not going to despoil our rivers with unsupervised dredging and mercury poisoning of our drinking water. We will raise taxes on claims producing over $20,000 in precious metal and there'll be a graduated tax on claims producing $100,000. These taxes will go toward building a city hospital and reducing the homeless population. We need to build better roads but not in far flung locations devoid of people. Our infrastructure such as sidewalks, bridges and roads need repair as our population soars. We need to improve transportation. I plan to establish committees to study all these issues and make recommendations. My first priority is the safety of our citizens and the need to get a handle on the rampant lawlessness that threatens our city. Elect me mayor and I'll get these things done. I've ministered to your souls as pastor, I'm a graduate of Yale University and I know how to get things done. I would be honored to be your next mayor."

# Chapter XI

It was a sunny, sparkling frigid day. The town's people were gathered in clusters around their favorite team. Some broke out in song, while others feted the driver of their favorite team with a veritable feast. Bookmakers ambled through the crowd quoting the odds on the different teams. Johnny had drawn the number twenty-eight. Margie pinned it on his back. Chuck went over the pit stops where the supplies were hidden for Johnny and the dogs. A number of people from his church came over to Johnny and wished him well. Chuck had strung up a number of campaign placards around the starting area knowing few events could draw a crowd like the race from Juneau to Pine Log.

Sue had drawn the number twelve. Johnny walked over to her. He could tell her team was strong by the two lead dogs. They were straining the reigns and had to be held back by two big men. The incessant barking nearly drowned out conversation.

Soapy Smith was surrounded by his entourage. Sue said, "I would keep my distance from him, Johnny, he's capable of anything. He has a number of henchmen who are out on the trail probably creating havoc as we speak."

"Thanks for the warning, Sue. I'm prepared for any shenanigans he may be up to. Eliminating me before Election Day is not beyond him. Miss Brown, how about a little wager. I'll bet my team against yours. Should I lose you get my claim. If I win you'll cease dredging the Cripple River and promise not to set up that rig anywhere on the river for two years. Is it a bet?"

"You've got a wager, Johnny," said Sue as she removed her mittens to vigorously shake his hand.

The area started to swell with people. The start of the race began in fifteen minutes. Johnny returned to his sled and thought about the impulsive wager he had just made. It was the only thing that could stop the dredging and preserve the river. Now he had to win. There was no turning back.

Mayor Biggs mounted the stand and gave a speech about the history of the Juneau to Pine Log Race. He recounted the thrilling finishes of the last three races and announced the new, larger prize money being offered this year. The people gave Sue Brown a rousing hand of applause for her generosity. Biggs' voice could hardly be heard above the hundreds of barking dogs. Johnny held the gang line with all his strength. The dogs were frantic with energy. Johnny noticed Tekla had bitten through his line and was now tangled up with Sweetpea and Ruffin. Johnny had Willie hold the lines while he waded among the dogs and tried to untangle the mess.

"And now may I remind you, the first sled to reach the halfway point at Kinnock will receive $20,000 in gold coins. Are you ready teams?" yelled Mayor Biggs above the din. "Good Luck! The Juneau to Pine Log Race is officially underway." A roar went up when the pistol went off. Johnny was replacing the tether when Sue went by him effortlessly. "Need help?" he could hear her ask as his ears reddened. He waved her off and angrily re-knotted the tether lines.

"Hurry, Johnny," shouted Willie Annue, "I don't think I can hold the dogs any longer."

"Mister Brady is having trouble with his team," announced Mayor Biggs.

"Come on, Johnny, get going," yelled the crowd.

Johnny bounded out amongst the harnessed dogs and took the gang line from Willie. "Go Dragon!"

"Hurry, Johnny, the lead team has a half mile on you," yelled Willie.

The dogs lurched forward with an explosive start. Johnny jumped on the drivers step and let the team whisk him off. The dogs were happy to be off and running. Their progress was swift as they passed two teams and came abreast of a third. The two teams raced for a half mile until Johnny yelled, "Pass, Titan!" Titan and Dragon responded and the sled easily accelerated passed the third team. The team continued at a moderate pace until they saw another team a quarter mile ahead. The other team gave the whip to his dogs and the sound caused Johnny's team to speed up until they were right along-side the other team. The dogs seemed to enjoy each other's company until Johnny yelled, "Pass Titan!"

The driver again whipped his team, but Titan and Dragon lurched forward and passed the team. The other driver grew frustrated and again whipped his team to no avail. Johnny was happy his team responded to his verbal cues. He hoped to save the whip until the stretch drive into Pine Log. He had worked long and hard to train his team to respond to his verbal cues and it paid off.

The dogs climbed a long steep hill. Johnny spoke to them constantly, urging them on. Once atop the hill, they raced and sometimes slid down the icy pass. The sled started to skid sideways. Johnny tried slowing them down but the slope was too steep. The sled started to slide awkwardly, pulling the team to the right. The path grew icier. The sled went into a long slide, and toppled over. The dogs tumbled into each other. Johnny jumped from the sled when he felt it about to tumble over. He landed in a snowbank as the sled and dogs went over and over. The dogs yelped and sat in a confused torpor as the tangled gang line hindered their movement. Johnny ran to the overturned sled.

What a fine start this was: two mishaps and not even ten miles from the start. I can't blame it on anybody. A spell of warm weather had melted parts of the trail which had later iced over. Johnny checked the sled over for broken parts and to see if any tools or supplies had been thrown off. He was happy to see the sled had withstood damage. The big problem was the time it was going to take to rearrange the tether lines. The dogs seemed to be free of injury. They barked and wagged their tails, happy to see him. Johnny untangled the lines. The dogs were eager to run. They seemed to sense they had some catching up to do.

"Go, Titan! Faster!" yelled Johnny. The dogs loped along for fifteen miles before they came abreast of another sled. When he passed the other team he notched a mark on the handle to remind himself of the number of teams ahead of him. The dogs made good progress as they loped along the Cripple River as it winded north. Johnny noticed how the gang line holding Dragon had been almost bitten through and was about to snap. Dragon had probably tried to free himself when the sled tumbled down the hill. Johnny was hesitant to stop them now because they were making good time on the river course.

He hoped they could hold out another hour or so until they made their first rest stop. While the dogs refreshed themselves he would fix the line. Looking ahead he could see his team was rapidly gaining on a team that had stopped. As he neared the team he saw the driver throw his gloves down in disgust. His dogs refused to budge.

"What happened?" asked Johnny.

"Ice between their paws! They won't move," retorted the despondent driver.

Johnny knew he was a first time racer. He failed to make booties for his team. Ice had hardened in their paws and each step became agony. Johnny was angry at the driver for failing to protect his team. People were blinded by the prize money and were driven by pure greed. The condition and care of the dogs throughout the race would determine the eventual winner. Now the man would have to wrap the paws of each dog and nurse them back to Juneau.

It began to snow. Johnny figured he had covered roughly thirty-five miles. The team was slowing to a trot. They were panting for food and water but were ten miles from their first scheduled stop. The gang line holding Dragon finally gave way and Johnny had to take several minutes to repair it. He spoke to the dogs, roughly petting each one as he fed them a dough ball laden with lard and meat. This was their first snack and they barked for more. "Let's go!" yelled Johnny as he saw another sled coming into view down in the valley.

It began to snow heavily. The winds picked up and pretty soon the trail was hidden from view. Johnny put Sweetpea into the lead with Taboo. Sweetpea could pick up a scent unlike any dog Johnny had ever known. When a small child was lost in the mountains near Juneau two years ago, Sweetpea found him under a tree and stayed with him as he howled for the searchers.

In a short while they came up to two other sleds trying to break trail. Johnny volunteered his team for the lead. This was one time in the race where everybody worked together. The snow was rapidly covering the trail and visibility was less than ten feet. The side winds had thrown the other dogs off course.

Sweetpea was the only one able to cut a straight trail.

The snow and winds continued unabated. After several hours Johnny reached his first rest stop. He left the others to continue on while he fed his famished dogs. He changed the booties on his team. He then dug a hole and pulled a large pot up. Inside was the special meal Margie, Joe and Millie had prepared for the dogs and a much smaller pot for himself. The dog's dough balls were laden with lard, meat and vitamins. The balls had been wrapped in burlap and were still soft. Johnny opened a covered dish that had been placed on top of the pot. It was spaghetti and meatballs prepared as only Millie Paoli could do. Johnny started a small fire and heated the meal. He then took the large pot and filled it with snow which he melted and gave to the dogs. They drank thirstily and then sat down while they waited for Johnny to finish his meal.

Johnny placed Sweetpea and Titan in the lead and the team departed. They soon caught up with other teams who were still breaking trail through the wind and snow. Johnny's team took the lead and easily broke trail for the rest. The snow and wind soon died down and the teams broke away. Within an hour, Johnny's team had passed the other three and was strongly racing uphill as they entered Treacherous Valley, an area known for devastating avalanches. They followed a winding river. Johnny looked up and saw several figures furtively running along the ridge. He urged the dogs on faster fearing he was about to be inundated with tons of snow.

The valley echoed with a thunderous explosion. Half the mountain seemed to break off and began a slow motion hurtle to the floor below. Johnny used his whip on the dogs. The dogs seemed to sense the avalanche as they dashed forward in an all-out effort to escape the roaring wall of snow. Trees snapped like toothpicks as the wall of snow roared down the valley. Only seconds saved them from certain death as the mountain fell behind the racing dogs. Powdered snow covered Johnny and the team. He dared not look back as he urged the team on. Surely this was the work of Soapy Smith and his gang. He probably knew the close finishers of last year's race and was going to try and pick them off, one by one. Johnny was grateful for the responsiveness of his team. All the hard training had been worth it. Completely clear of the avalanche, he stopped his team and surveyed the damage. The entrance to the valley was completely hidden from sight. The tops of tall pines were peeking through the new cover of snow like buttons on a jacket.

Gazing on the mountainous ridges, where the avalanche was born, Johnny could see three small specks moping about. He knew he was dealing with men who would stop at nothing. He untied the sack that carried essentials he would need for the race. At the bottom was a small Colt revolver. He unloaded six shells from a box and fed them into the revolver's chamber. Jim Fenwick had given him the gun over his protests when he learned Soapy Smith had entered the race. Johnny tucked the revolver in a small side pocket of his leather parka. He urged the team on until they rose out of the valley and on to the open plains.

He followed a marker pointing out the direction to Finger Lake. Tekla began limping so Johnny loaded him aboard the sled to prevent further injury. The team continued on till late afternoon. Johnny began to sense something was wrong when they still hadn't reached Finger Lake. He saw another team coming in the opposite direction.

"Turn back! Somebody switched the markers! We're at least ten miles off course!"

"Oh no," groaned Johnny, "That explains everything. Now I've got to make up twenty miles. What else can go wrong? A bad start, an avalanche, and now somebody switched the markers." Looking up to the sky, Johnny shrugged his shoulders and asked for patience.

When Johnny reached the other teams he told them of the avalanche and of seeing three men on the ridge. They raced along for several miles then Johnny's team shot away at the point of their misdirection. He urged his team on at a jogging pace. They responded to his command as the evening turned to dusk. Johnny turned on his headlamp. It shone ahead for about twenty yards. The team seem to race for the beam, never catching it. "I'm in luck; if they keep this pace up I can make up some lost ground." Tekla was in the sled barking away, encouraging the team on. Johnny worked the team through the night. He gave up a rest spot in an attempt to gain some ground. He knew he was forcing the dogs, but they seemed to respond. Good thing he had done some sixty mile jaunts with them in training because they were going to stretch it to the limit tonight.

Around midnight he faintly saw the beam of another sled a half mile away. The dogs were slowing. It took about a half hour before he came abreast of the other sled. Silently the other driver whipped his team into a sprint. Johnny's team seemed to enjoy running abreast of another team. Losing the other's presence sparked them into a sprint. After about a mile they came abreast of another driver. Johnny had never seen him before. He could see the agitation in his eyes of being caught by Johnny's team. For a half mile they stayed even with each other. Johnny gave a verbal command and the team responded on cue. Johnny was so pleased with his dogs. They went into a sprint and rapidly outpaced the other driver. Johnny was tired but his dogs seemed to have energy left.

He let the dogs have their way. He figured they had covered sixty-five miles since the race began. At one time his team picked up the outline of a startled moose. The dogs barked incessantly and started off after the moose. Johnny pulled on the tether line and got them back on the trail. They continued along for several more miles before Johnny brought them to a halt. He took out his supply map and checked for his buried supplies.

He knew he had passed a pit stop and wanted to make sure the team was fed and new boots put on their paws. He could barely make out a mountain pass up ahead in the moonlit night. Food supplies, booties and medicine were hidden at the end of the mountain pass. They still had four to five miles to go. The dogs loped slowly. Johnny could tell fatigue was setting in. He kept up a chatty banter with his team and he made sure to compliment each dog by name for the job they had done. They responded by turning their heads as if to say you're welcome. The uphill climb to the mountain pass was difficult and slow going. Johnny stopped for a while and put Tekla as the lead dog. The rest he'd been given proved worthwhile. He pulled the rest of the team through the mountain pass. The other dogs responded to his energy and loped along.

Johnny looked for two large boulders spaced about five feet apart. He saw them up ahead. The team stopped at the spot while Johnny dug up the rations. He fed his dogs the lard balls filled with meat. Tekla ate voraciously. He melted snow over a fire for drinking water. After the dogs had eaten, he called them over to a large, spreading pine. He playfully tugged at each one and commanded them to rest.

He ate his own meal of hash and eggs and then crawled under the huge pine to try and sleep. It began to snow. The pine offered good shelter for the exhausted dogs, for in minutes they were fast asleep. Johnny took out his map and looked over the terrain they would be covering tomorrow. He identified trouble spots where he might be vulnerable to Soapy Smith and his gang. He put away the map and laid his head back on the soft pine matting. In minutes he was fast asleep.

Johnny woke to the barking of his dogs. It appeared that they were still hungry. He fed them the remaining lard balls and gave them strips of leather to chew on while he made coffee and breakfast for himself. It had snowed several inches during the night, but this morning was bright and beautiful. He wondered where Sue Brown was about now. He hoped Soapy Smith and his gang hadn't harmed her. Good thing she had brought a couple of bodyguards with her. The outlaws were capable of anything.

He gathered his bedroll and utensils and stored them in the sled. He attached the tether line to his team. He put Titan and Sweetpea as the lead dogs. The dogs were barking in anticipation of the run. He knew he had to make up a lot of mileage today in order to get back in the race. He estimated the lead team had a forty mile head start on him. The dog's barking reverberated through the mountain pass as Johnny sent them into a jog. "Git, you dogs! We've got some catching up to do!"

Once through the mountain pass and out on the open plains they came to a marker pointing to Snedecker's Landing. It followed a river course. To the right was a dense forest of pine, to the left the river. He couldn't find any evidence that other teams had been this way before. He tried several spots, still no trail. He walked to his right thinking a trail might be carved and brushed away the new snow. Sure enough, the crusted snow below had been broken and his fingers could feel the outline of a sled's runner. Someone had tampered with the markers during the night.

Johnny drove the team toward the forest. As he neared the forest a natural opening denoting a trail could be seen. He was now on level ground so he let the dogs run as fast as they could. An hour later he pulled the team up to an outpost that featured a general store and several cabins. So this was Snedecker's Landing. A pen nearby held several howling dogs, probably left there because they were disabled in some way. Johnny tied his team to a hitching post and went inside. Sally Koi and her husband owned the general store. Snedecker's Landing had been built when rich deposits of platinum were discovered in the 1880's. The vein had been worked to exhaustion then abandoned after an earthquake struck and collapsed the mine shaft. Sally and her husband now served a large Eskimo population. They bought furs from the Eskimos up north and traded food stuff, clothing and other necessities as barter.

Johnny warmed himself by a roaring fire. He gave Sally a list of items he needed. Her husband went outside and gave the dogs snacks made from seal meat and fish. Sally gave Johnny a cup of hot coffee and told him the last team had passed through an hour or so earlier. The first team had passed through twelve hours ago.

He told her of the trouble caused by changed markers and the avalanche. She remembered three men stopping by on horseback and described them to Johnny. She was a bit afraid of them. They seemed to have hostile intentions but Sally's husband had been cleaning a rifle when they came in. They bought some baling wire and a number of shovels and left in a hurry.

Johnny went outside and checked the paws of all the dogs. He put medicinal salve on any that looked raw or cracking and wrapped them in new booties. After he packed his supplies in the tent he said goodbye to his host and took off for the next leg of the journey. It would be a twenty mile trek across the Peck Glacier. It was the most dangerous part of the race. The glacier was filled with rifts and ridges and deep abysses. It was going to be a test of strength for the dogs.

Progress was slow. To make matters worse it began to snow. There were markers at quarter mile intervals. If he was going to get lost on a glacier, the odds of ever being found were slim. Howling winds made visibility impossible. The dogs just groped ahead. Fifteen foot high ridges sometimes made the dogs slide back. They would muster their strength and continue ahead.

It was then that Johnny heard the faint sound of dogs barking and wailing. It was coming from up ahead. They mounted one ridge, then another. Over the third ridge they saw a huge rift in the ice. A faint human cry emanated from below. Johnny stopped the team and anchored them away from the abyss. "My God, a team had fallen through a crevasse," he thought to himself. He approached the edge with caution and could hear faint cries from a female. He raced back to his sled and got his lantern. He lit it and held it over the abyss. The swirling of wind driven snow made visibility difficult. During a pause in the wind Johnny could see a figure writhing in pain about fifty feet down the crevasse. She was prone on a narrow ledge, inches away from the abyss. The only thing preventing her from falling was the overturned sled wedged upside down. One of the dogs had struggled atop the sled and was howling in pain. The others had slipped from their harness and had fallen to their deaths. As Johnny hollered he saw Sue Brown clutching her right leg.

The sled was slowly slipping deeper into the crevasse because of the frantic dog's weight. Sue's leg had gotten caught in the tether line and she was being drawn into the crevasse with every movement of the sled. "You've got to cut the tether line, Sue!" yelled Johnny before racing off to his sled and pulling a coil of rope from storage. He made a loop and lowered it down the crevasse. He told her to loop it around her body. He pulled on the rope but there was no give as she yelled in pain.

"I'm going down, stay calm." He drove a piton in the hard pack ice and looped it around several times. He now had two ropes to deal with. He began to descend down the crevasse. Several times he tried to get a foothold but the wall was a sheet of ice. "Hurry, Johnny, the sled is sinking deeper!"

Johnny watched as the dog shifted his weight and the movement sent the sled careening forward, pitching the dog into the abyss. Sue screamed as she was suspended over the crevasse, saved only by the rope encircling her body. Her body went limp as she fainted in fright. Johnny grabbed for the loop and began pulling her up slowly, locking in each movement every few feet. "That was a close call, if I had gotten here fifteen minutes later she'd be a goner," he thought to himself. Reaching the top, he scrambled out and pulled her from the crevasse.

He started a fire and heated a tin of water. He held Sue in his arms to keep her as warm as possible. She awoke and cried out. Seeing Johnny she whispered. "You appeared out of nowhere and saved me. I've been down there for hours. When the sled fell through I hit my head and was out. Seeing you now is like looking into the face of a guardian angel. Johnny, I was so scared." She hid her face in his parka and sobbed. He gently stroked her hair.

"It's O.K. now, you're safe. What happened?" asked Johnny.

49

"I was near the lead, I moved off the trail because a ridge was impassable. Then the ice gave way and we tumbled into the crevasse. I screamed and yelled and a short time later a man appeared over the opening. I thought he was going to help me, but he just laughed and went away. I think it was Soapy Smith. He had this cruel laugh," said Sue as she sipped the hot tea Johnny handed to her.

"It probably was. Some of his own men started an avalanche and moved several markers. That's why I was delayed getting here. In retrospect, it was a good thing they hindered me. I came just in time. How did you become separated from your bodyguards?"

"When we came to Snedecker's Landing, I told them they could leave because they were slowing me down. Two hours later I fell through the crevasse. Do you think Soapy and his gang will win the race?" asked Sue.

"I'm not sure; a lot of good teams left Juneau. Now let me set that leg...it looks like it was tangled up pretty bad from what I could see." Johnny rolled up her pant leg and pushed down the heavy wool socks. A large bruised area was exposed. Johnny put pressure on the bottom of her foot. She screamed in agony. "I think your leg may be fractured."

"Damn! What a fine mess this is. I sponsored a race and break my leg. I guess it could have been worse. I could have lost my life if you hadn't come along. It's ironic, you oppose everything I stand for, and now I'm indebted to you for saving my life," said Sue as she looked into Johnny's brown eyes.

Johnny went about making a splint for her leg. He broke several branches from a tree and whittled them down until they were smooth. He wrapped them in fur skin and gently placed the splints on each side of her leg.

He pulled down her pant leg and bound the leg with rope.

"Did you hear me, Johnny? I owe you for my life. I know I've been a thorn in your side and now I want to make amends. What can I do to repay you for saving my life?"

"Do you really want to do something that will make a difference? You wield plenty of power in Juneau. Having you by my side in the race for mayor would really bolster my campaign. Together we would make a difference in Juneau. With your connections to the business community I'd have support that would be hard to beat. If you'd help me, I'd be real grateful. That's a race worth running and winning. We could make a difference in a lot of lives."

She smiled happily then grimaced as the pain in her leg began to throb. Johnny cleared out the storage compartment as best he could and placed Sue in the sled. He placed soft packing beneath her head. "How's that," he asked.

"Fine, Johnny I'm sorry I've been so much trouble for you."

"You know, I'm beginning to think it was fate. It's so much better having you on my side then against me. Some races are worth winning. I want to make Juneau a great place to raise a family and it doesn't end there. I see a future for Alaska and possibly statehood some day. How did you wind up here in Juneau, Sue?"

"My father was an Irish immigrant who worked on the Canadian Railroad. He met a beautiful Italian girl in Vancouver. The railroad got a contract to build a connection to Alaska and to encourage employees to move, they gave land grants. He was one of the first settlers in Alaska and we had 160 acres of timber and streams. He built a warehouse for timber and shipped lumber to Canada. Then there was a gold rush and he foolishly left his business and began mining for gold. As his fortune diminished he began to drink heavily and gradually disappeared from the picture. It was my mother who raised me. She was a practical woman. I remember how she worked like a man to keep the timber business going, hiring lumberjacks. I remember the poverty of our existence. When my brother died I vowed to accomplish all the things he wanted to do as a tribute to my mother. My mother passed away a few years ago but not before seeing the dream she had wished for her children come true during her own lifetime."

"So that's what has driven you to succeed in a man's world?'" said Johnny as the team pushed the sled over a ridge.

"My mother taught me to believe in myself, to work harder than the other person and never stop learning. When she got old and had to abandon the timber business, she came to Juneau and started a small cafe. She told me that people would always need food and a place to sleep. When the gold rush started and people were coming from thousands of miles away, a banker who was enamored of me lent me several thousand dollars. I immediately had several hotels built. They were occupied overnight. I took the profits and borrowed more money and built more hotels and saloons. Men were willing to pay any price for the luxury of a warm bath, some good food, and a little company. Tell me about yourself, Johnny." asked Sue as the sled made its way up another ridge.

"Have you ever tried to contact your family?" asked Sue as the dogs strained to reach the top of another ridge.

"A friend of mine delivers letters and packages for me as he makes his way south toward San Francisco every year. Someday I'll go back to Indiana but my home is here now. Juneau has been good to me. I came here and managed to make a good life for myself. Now I have the opportunity to help others. My grandfather taught me to value wisdom and to never stop growing. Now look at me, I'm running for mayor, and I've just saved the most beautiful girl in Juneau. Life just can't get more exciting than that," said Johnny as he looked down at Sue.

He found himself with a renewed admiration for this plucky girl who rose up from obscurity and who had achieved so much. He wondered why she had never married. "Sue, I know you're younger than me. Don't you ever get lonely and want to settle down and have a family?"

"Yea, sometimes I think about it. But usually I'm too busy running my business. At times I think I'm running away from involvement because I don't want to tie myself up. The man I marry would have to be mighty interesting. I get bored easily. He'd have to put up with an independent woman, someone who is used to getting her own way. Not many men would like to settle down with a woman like that. Am I right?"

"You're a beautiful woman, Sue. You can be mighty aggressive when you're after something. And you don't mince words; you say what's on your mind. The reason I never settled down was because I never completely felt at home here. Lately however, I begun to realize this is my home and I want to make it a livable place. My friends are all here and being of Irish heritage makes little difference to them. I can't offer much except my hope and aspirations for the future, my interest in politics and a nice little house on the Cripple River."

"Are you proposing to me, Johnny?" asked Sue.

"Could you see yourself settling down with a man like me, Sue? I think I'm ready for commitment and change in my life. You could do worse. I have lots of interests and I could make a living being mayor. With you on my side in the race for mayor, we could make an unbeatable team," said Johnny feeling and thinking thoughts he'd never thought he could express.

"Johnny, are you asking me to marry you?" asked Sue.

"I don't want to take advantage of you. You could think about it. You're in a bad state now, feeling kind of beholden to me for saving your life. But if you could see yourself saying *yes*, you'd make me mighty happy," said Johnny as they left the glacier and entered a smoother trail.

"Yes."

"Did you say *yes*, I mean really *yes*, you'd marry me?" said Johnny, his heart racing with joy.

"I did."

Johnny stopped the sled, sat down on the snow and looked into her eyes. "Sue, do you know what you're saying? You've just made me the happiest man in the world. I've been meaning to say that I've loved you a long time. You are the only woman who has held a power over me. I never could explain it. It was the power to hurt, the power to uplift, the power to make a man feel uneasy," he took off his glove and caressed her cheek with his hand.

"And you could make me so mad and sad too, Johnny. Sad especially when I said things to hurt you. I just wanted you to feel. I wanted to break through that calm exterior of yours and make you feel something. I wanted to shatter that peace of mind you presented to the world. Maybe I envied you. I've never been able to feel complacent about anything. There was always something to achieve, to make up for. Even though I had a lot of material possessions, I always felt something was missing. I sensed you weren't driven like me, but you were at peace with yourself."

"Sue, you were right. I was too complacent with myself. I began to see the world through your eyes and realized I had to get involved in resolving some of the problems of the community I lived in. You have to work for solutions to the problems in our community," said Johnny. "My grandfather, who was a great leader of his people, had taught me that by example. Somehow I'd forgotten the lesson that his principles came out of his love for his people and family," said Johnny.

"When I am with you, Johnny, there are no problems, only solutions and a feeling of wholeness. I don't feel driven, except to make you happy," said Sue, blushing.

"And when I'm with you a whole new world of possibilities open up before me. I feel so strong and so much in love." He kissed her cheek.

She enveloped him in her arms in an ardent embrace. They found love, the greatest prize in the race.

# CHAPTER XII

They arrived in Juneau three days later at one in the morning. Johnny had been forced to take shelter in a snow cave he dug out for the sled team. Nearby were the remains of food and lard balls he had hidden away on the trek out. It was a habit he had learned in an earlier race when he had been forced to turn back. Planning for any eventuality had paid off. They could have starved to death from the lack of food and energy had he not found the cache.

Sue was in bad shape. Her leg had begun to swell from the pounding of going over an ice field. An ugly purple welt began to spread upward from the calf area. Red lines radiated from it. Johnny knew he had to get her into Juneau fast. The blizzard had continued for days. Johnny fed the team from the meager remains of the last lard ball. The howling winds blew drifts that covered the entrance to the snow cave.

By the time they arrived in Juneau, Sue no longer had feeling in her leg. Johnny raced passed the offices of several medical men known for filling the cemeteries on the outskirts of town with their deceased patients. A few of these doctors were veterinarians, but because Juneau couldn't attract qualified physicians, the town folks accepted their ministering to their health needs. "All mammals are the same, ain't they?" said Dr. Smithson as he changed his practice "To caring for the health needs of the human animal."

Johnny drove the team toward Dr. Fred's house. Dr. Fred had served the people of Juneau for over forty years. He graduated from Columbia University Medical

School in New York. He had been a battlefield medic during the American Civil War and had seen much carnage. President Lincoln became appalled at the losses to staph infection from even minor injuries. He ordered his commanders to send the best of their medics to New York for training in the latest surgical techniques. The army paid for his medical education. Three months later Lee surrendered at Appomattox. While at Columbia, Dr. Fred had fallen in love with a Canadian nurse. He traveled to Juneau to meet her family and stayed to fight an epidemic of typhus. He was the only doctor for two hundred miles until the veterinarian came in during the gold rush.

Dr. Fred Grace answered the pounding on his door. "Johnny, what brings you here?"

"It's Miss Brown, Dr. Fred. She fell into a snow crevice during the Pine Log Race. I think she broke her leg. She's in a bad way," he rasped as he pulled the stretcher from the sled.

"Bring her in here Johnny. The poor girl is freezing," said Dr. Fred as they both lifted the stretcher and brought her into the den where a crackling fire had warmed the room. The radiant heat from the fireplace made Johnny aware, for the first time, of how cold he had been during the journey. He held his numbed hands over the fireplace while Dr. Fred examined Sue. Dr. Fred was in his seventies. A lifetime of caring and dealing with death and disease was reflected in the creases and worry lines that marked his face.

"Maria," he bellowed. "Get some hot tea and food. We have guests. It's John Brady and Sue Brown."

A tall, dark-haired woman in her late fifties came into the room with a tray of hot bread, cheese and sausages. She greeted Johnny warmly, walked to her husband's side and gently caressed Sue's face. "You poor dear," she said as she took in the extent of her injuries. "How did it happen?"

"During the race to Pine Log somebody switched trail markers. I was led into a mountainous valley. A volley of gunshots set off an avalanche that nearly buried my team. Once out of the valley I was directed by trail markers into Glacier Bay, that's where the team fell into a crevice. Why would someone want to kill me, Johnny?" asked Sue as she grimaced from the shooting pain in her leg.

"Could be for the prize money," said Johnny. "Soapy Smith and his gang have been known to kill for a lot less reason. Somehow I think there's more to it, you must have something he wants and you're standing in his way," said Johnny as he held Sue's hand. Dr. Fred was now bandaging the leg wound and applying iodine to the infection.

"You know Johnny, while you were away Judge Kerr invalidated your petition. The mayor challenged your petition drive. He put pressure on a number of people who signed it to change their story and swear that they were misled. Pass me that sponge, Johnny," said Dr. Fred as he cleaned away the blood around the wound.

"Don't tell me Judge Kerr is against me, too! I always figured him as a fair man."

"It's politics, Johnny. It was the mayor who appointed Kerr, so now he's calling in his favors. You'll have to go before him for a hearing to reinstate the petition drive. There, that should do it, Sue. You have to keep off your feet for a couple of weeks, but I think we halted the infection. Another day or so, it would have been gangrene and I'd have to amputate. You're a lucky girl, Sue."

"Lucky Johnny came along when he did," said Sue as she looked into his eyes.

"Don't worry, Sue. No one is going to hurt you; never again. I'll get to the bottom of this. I've got friends here in the sheriff's office who'll post a guard round the clock if I ask them. In the morning I'll see Judge Kerr. Now you've got to rest. Doc, do you think she could stay here a day or so until I get things in order for her?"

"Sure, Johnny, Marie will make things cozy for her right here. And don't worry about her being safe here. Toby will take care of her security. Marie, where's Toby? Before she could respond a huge German Shepard put both paws on Dr. Fred's chest and licked his face.

"Get down, Toby! We got a guest here tonight. Anybody snooping around, you take care of it, O.K.?" said Dr. Fred as he cleaned and filed away his instruments. The dog wagged his tail as if he understood and walked to the front door and gently lowered his huge body to assume his sentry duties.

Johnny kissed Sue, thanked the doctor and his wife and gently exited the door, making sure not to perturb the sentry on duty.

Outside in the brisk, frigid air his team eagerly awaited his coming. They rose in unison and responded promptly to his command. Johnny headed toward Juneau. He decided to spend the night in a room Margie Upak had in her Japanese restaurant. Since she sponsored him, he owed her an explanation. Margie, being a romantic would say he'd won a greater prize, Sue Brown's heart.

As he was passing through Juneau, he saw a light still burning in Chuck Harris' blacksmith shop. He tied the team to a stable post and told them to be quiet. They settled their bodies into the new fallen snow and chewed at their ice encrusted paws while Johnny entered the shop.

"Johnny! I thought you'd be in Pine Log by now," said Chuck Harris rising from shoeing a mule.

Johnny told him what had happened during the race.

"Well, how is she now?" asked Chuck as he wiped his huge hands on a leather apron.

"She's at Doc Grace's house; she's hurtin' from a bad leg injury."

"Johnny, if you add what you just told me to what happened to the sheriff, we got big problems in Juneau."

"What happened to Sheriff Goldring?"

"That's right, you wouldn't know. Terrible thing; never had a chance. He was called out to settle a claim dispute when he was shot in the face. We buried him yesterday. Turns out one of Soapy Smith's men was intimidating a miner. Sheriff was bringing the man in when he lunged for his gun. They wrestled but the man managed to grab the sheriff's gun and shoot him. A deputy killed the man."

"That does it! I've made up my mind. To hell with the race for mayor! What this town needs now is a good sheriff! Could you start up a petition for me Chuck? We got only eight days before the election. I'm mad as hell with what they did to Sue Brown and now the sheriff. I've been a preacher man a good part of my life, but I just can't sit around anymore waiting for the other guy to take care of my problems."

"Johnny, you must be crazy. What experience do you have in keeping the peace? Why you hate guns. How you gonna handle all the rowdies, Johnny, that come into this town? And that's not counting the prospectors up in the hills; why there's a killing or two taking place everyday up there," said Chuck as he wiped the grime from a smithy's work on his denim apron.

"I'll get me some good men as deputies but when I don't like a man and he needs to be brought to justice, I like to look him in the face before I disable him or, God forbid, have to kill him. I have an old Chinese friend named Huang Lee who taught me the art of Kung Fu. I've never had to use it because I'm a peaceful man, who likes to talk, but lately the bad guys have been winning too much and this once beautiful city of Juneau is their prize. They aim to take it over, lock, stock and barrel and they ain't too subtle about it," said Johnny as he looked down at both of his hands as if they had a life of their own.

"I'll get started on the petitions right away, Johnny. I don't give you much of a chance to win but we'll see what happens."

"I'm going to call in a lot of favors I did for the citizens of Juneau. The prospectors are mostly from the States and I've got a good relationship with their leaders, me having a claim of my own. Most of the prospectors don't vote, but if I can get them out, I'd have a better chance," said Johnny. "I'll be leaving now, Chuck. File those petitions as soon as you can. We gotta squeeze in a lot of campaigning in the next seven days. I'll get my people to arrange the stops and provide the refreshments. That reminds me. I gotta stop over at Margie Upak's place and break the bad news."

"What bad news?"

"She backed me in the race to Pine Log. Entry fee, the best mush team, and larder for the pit stops. I guess I let her down, didn't even finish the race."

"Johnny, you know Margie, she likes you and her heart is made of gold. She knows you're a winner even though you lost a measly race. You saved Sue didn't you? Sue ain't gonna forget it, either. So don't worry, Johnny, Margie never makes an investment that doesn't bring her a good return. She's patient, kind and shrewd. I oughta know; she lent me the seed money that allowed me to expand this shop five years ago. With Margie on your team in the race for sheriff, maybe we could win. While you're there, ask about the chef, I think he'd make a good deputy," said Chuck suppressing a laugh. He was demonstrating something called Karate to a couple of kids behind Margie's restaurant when a few of the fellas from the Last Chance Saloon staggered into the backyard and decided to introduce American boxing to the chef. All four of them rushed him at once. They were out cold when I heard the commotion and rushed back there. The kids were so impressed they got Kyoto giving classes twice a week in the Knights of Columbus Hall in downtown Juneau. The kids claim Kyoto once held off eighty men when he got caught in a riot in Chinatown. He was buying vegetables for Margie in the Chinese market when all hell broke loose. The men advanced on him but retreated when five of the men suffered broken bones in the melee. He's the kind of man you could use, Johnny."

"Can't wait to meet him, thanks Chuck," said Johnny as he left the smithy shop. "Karate," he mumbled to himself as he untied the dogs and mounted the sled. With a little Kung Fu and a dash of Karate I think we just might be able to bring some order to the territories, thought Johnny as the team's barking broke the silence of the cold, white night.

# CHAPTER XIII

Mayor Biggs was reelected mayor in a landslide. Soapy Smith contributed $100,000 to his campaign after convincing him to run for one more time. Biggs dismissed the three party hacks he had designated mayoral candidates with a wave of his hand and a consolation prize of $1,000 each for standing in for him until the big money from Soapy came through. He had hoped more reputable concerns would have come forward with a major contribution, but $100,000 was a $100,000. Not to be dismissed lightly.

On a personal level Mayor Biggs disliked Soapy Smith immensely. He was uncouth, foul-mouthed, vile smelling and he reeked of whiskey. The fact that he shot a bullet into the ceiling while Biggs was outlining his campaign plans caused great anxiety to the distinguished gathering of party hacks to the Juneau Free Democratic Convention. His words were etched into Biggs' memory:

"Uh, Mayor Biggs you can desist with the flowery oratory cause I'll be telling you what the campaign plans are. Everyone holding a claim within thirty miles of Juneau City will be paying a city prospectors fee of ten percent on all their earnings. This will be used to pay for roads and sewerage into the mountains and far-flung hamlets of our great city. Right boys!" said Soapy turning to his grimy entourage of political supporters seated around him. "We're with you, Soapy!" they cried out in unison. A few of the more rambunctious supporters raised their guns and were about to fire into the ceiling when Soapy cast a baleful glance their way.

"I'll be leading the parade here, gentlemen" he shouted as he drew his Colt .45. "From now on you smelly, whiskey laden criminals will clean up your act or else! The citizens of Juneau will demand no less! Isn't that right, Mr. Biggs!" said Soapy as his entourage quickly holstered their guns and sheepishly smiled at his every word.

"You're correct, sir. As I was saying in my campaign speech, the citizens of Juneau will demand no less than absolute adherence to my campaign plans!" said Soapy drowning out the cowering Biggs with his booming voice. "Isn't that right Mayor?" said Soapy swinging his Colt revolver toward Biggs' direction. "The collection of city taxes will commence on the 2nd of January. We want the citizens to have a Happy New Year. The prospector's tax along with license fees for all businesses plus a liquor tax will be due at the end of January. Those failing to pay these taxes by April 15th will be sentenced by Judge Kerr to thirty days in jail. We will begin construction on a road network into the far-flung hamlets that will be halted because of lack of funds; we will then raise taxes..."

John Brady was elected sheriff by the slimmest of margins, edging out Racey Williams, the former sheriff of Pine Log who appeared in Juneau suddenly one day announcing his candidacy. "I am throwing my hat in the ring at the urging of the honorable and esteemed Soapy Smith. I've been a Republican all my life and, after bringing law and order to Pine Log, I felt it was my duty to put a stop to the plague of violence and chicanery that has invaded the once proud city of Juneau. When a "foreigner with a fancy college education" from a stateside village announced his candidacy as sheriff, I was appalled that the good citizens of Juneau would even entertain the thought that a Black Irishman could maintain order in their fair city..."

It looked like Racey Williams was gonna win until mush drivers returning from the Pine Log Race revealed that Racey had suddenly left town after he had impregnated two young widows, left bereft of money and sympathy after their prospector husbands were killed while working their claims. Racey had befriended Soapy while Soapy was held in the Pine Log jail on suspicion in the killings. Soapy had been released from jail; the next day the headlines read: "Mayor Publicly Apologizes to Mr. Smith for Wrongful Jailing. Smith Donates $100,000 toward New Jail." A photo appeared showing Soapy handing $100,000 in gold nuggets to the mayor. Racey could be seen beaming with gratitude at the benevolent Mr. Soapy Smith.

Johnny held a party for his campaign committee at Joe and Millie Paola's Italian restaurant . In seven days of intensive campaigning, Joe, Millie, Jim Ewing, Margie, Willie Annue, Sister Thomas, Jim Fenwick and Judge Brownstein had covered the city in a nonstop campaign to elect Johnny sheriff.

In three days they got the required signatures to get placed on the ballot. Johnny knew he'd won the election due to his friend's influence in the community. Each held a position of respect in the community so the victory was a personal victory in terms of their influence. Any doubt Johnny felt about fulfilling the duties of sheriff disappeared with the deep loyalty Johnny felt toward the sacrifices his friends had made on his behalf. He felt strong and complete in their presence.

The aroma of pasta, sausages, meatballs and ravioli permeated the air. Wine and laughter flowed freely as the committee recounted their campaign experiences with the prospectors in the hills. When Johnny heard some of the criticism the prospectors had voiced about his run for sheriff, he both laughed and silently resolved to overcome their cynicism and doubt. He knew he had to do something about anarchy and the law of the jungle that existed in the hills. To realize that his friends had succeeded in reaching thousands of outlying citizens of Juneau humbled him. Their banter, laughter and social commentary on conditions in outlying areas gave him a broader picture of the populace he was obligated to serve. Johnny got up to make a toast to his eight friends and the other supporters gathered in the kerosene and candlelit restaurants. A crackling fire warmed the room while a waiter serenaded the diners with sentimental Italian favorites. "Millie and Joe graciously opened their bistro on this cold, frigid night to celebrate our victory. I owe them and you more than I can say. For it is truly our victory. You felt that Juneau deserved better. You choose to get involved and not let the bad guys take over this town. I started my run for sheriff over the outrages committed against Sue Brown. Our relationship, mine and Sue, started out rocky. We differed about everything. But the one thing that unites us all here today is our outrage over offences against fair play and justice. When a woman who has given so much to the people becomes the target of evil men, that's where I draw the line.

I know you all pretty well. You know that Juneau is capable of a better future. Evil will not triumph here. It has raised its head and threatens the body which is the people. I believe in people and your belief in what people can accomplish brings us all here today. The people have made a choice and I mean to carry out their wishes. As of today, we're gonna have a peaceful city. I've picked my deputies and, starting tomorrow, we're going into training. Kyoto, Margie's chef is an expert in martial arts. He has agreed to teach us an ancient art of self-defense called Karate. Huang, an old friend of mine, is returning from San Francisco with a man skilled in Kung Fu.

There are too many bullets flying around Juneau. We need a return to unarmed combat. We will set the example by enforcing the law with the strength that God gave us. That means we gotta be stronger and quicker than the bad guys."

"Hold on, Johnny! How long do you think you'll last when a Colt .45 slug comes tearing into your heart? It's nice to have ideals and want to set an example but you gotta live in the real world, Johnny. An unarmed sheriff won't last three days here in Juneau. The gun rules in the hills. That's the only law there is," said Jim Ewing, speaking from seven years of police service as a Mountie.

"I didn't say we won't defend ourselves. If shot at, we will take appropriate action and deal a crushing counter attack to the perpetrator. We will discourage the use of firearms by not wearing them ourselves. Our demeanor when dealing with aggressive and hostile men will be not to upset them further, but to encourage them to settle the difference peacefully."

"Johnny, are we living in the same city! It's a jungle out there. Why just the other day, outside our restaurant, a prospector from the hills was shot dead. Some disagreement over a card game, I think," said Joe Paoli, brushing his hair back with his hand as he recalled the terrible scene of a man dying in agony, calling out the name of his wife or girlfriend. The sense of helplessness he felt as he tried to stem the flow of blood from a gaping wound would remain with him forever.

"That's the very thing I'm talking about. Too much of that occurs in Juneau. Too many orphans walk our streets, their fathers buried on Dawson Hill, victims on the losing side of gunfights, some just plain ambushed, their killers never found. I aim to put a stop to it and we can succeed if we try a new strategy; a strategy that has met success in the Orient. My friend, Huang, the tailor told me a story that I've never forgotten."

"About 600 years ago in China there lived an emperor who decreed that the populace must never be armed, he was afraid of being overthrown. He wanted his soldiers to be the only ones in possession of arms so that his family would live forever. He raided the people's houses and places of business and removed anything that looked like a weapon. He then raided Buddhist monasteries because they were for teaching the martial arts. The teachers were ousted and imprisoned. The emperor proved to be a cruel tyrant who terrorized the people."

Opposition to this rule came from an unlikely place. In a Shaolin temple, tucked away in the mountains, a Buddhist nun named Lee Shon developed Kung Fu, a martial art based on the teachings of the martial arts masters of the times, many of them Buddhists monks. Requiring only the use of hands and feet, speed and quickness, it soon proved to be lethal and very practical. Its use spread rapidly among the populace because Lee trained community leaders who taught others the secret of Kung Fu. Devoid of weapons to respond to the cruelty of the emperor, Lee taught the people how to turn ordinary farm implements into weapons utilizing Kung Fu motions and defensive principles. Within five years the farmers overthrew the emperor and his vast well-armed soldiers in mass uprisings. Kung Fu aided in the establishment of a more benevolent rule and soon took on a spiritual property because it had defeated the forces of evil in feudal China. Kung Fu still retains that spiritual aura today and legends have grown around the masters who practice it and promote its use. It builds character and self-discipline, traits sorely needed in Juneau today."

"So you're saying weapons are all around us, we just need to think about it? How about a demonstration of its effectiveness, Johnny?" said Willie Annue as he rose from the table. He withdrew a long fish knife, concealed in his coat. "How could you handle someone coming at you, with this baby?" asked Willie smiling. "You'd have to run, wouldn't you, Johnny?" he laughed as he returned the knife to its sheath and sat down.

"Maybe a demonstration is needed to convince you," said Johnny as he moved toward Willie. They cleared several tables and chairs and created an open space fifteen feet square. The guests looked on in anticipation not knowing earlier that Johnny had studied Kung Fu many years.

"Now Willie, come at me with that knife. Don't be shy; I won't hurt you but you'll be disarmed rapidly."

"Are you sure, Johnny? I'm pretty good with this baby. Been in a couple of scraps in my life."

"O.K.," Willie, let's do it."

Willie lunged toward Johnny. Johnny feigned a kick toward Willie's knife hand that caused Willie to draw back momentarily. In an instant he was in close. His left hand circled Willie's knife hand at the wrist. His right hand delivered three quick light blows to Willie's face that disoriented him. Johnny gave a twist to Willie's knife hand, the knife fell to the floor and Willie whirled past Johnny sprawled face first on the floor.

The assorted guests clapped in amazement at the speed and effectiveness of the lightening moves they had just witnessed. From the time Willie lunged and landed face first on the floor, less than two seconds had elapsed. Johnny helped Willie to his feet, apologizing for his fall. "I meant to keep you on your feet but your momentum was strong," said Johnny as he checked Willie's wrist.

"Johnny, that was great! How's it done? It was so quick and done with. I wanted to scare you by cutting a few buttons from your shirt, suddenly I was on the floor. It works, you convinced me," said Willie as he retrieved his knife and sat down.

"That's O.K. Johnny, when you're dealing with knives and people up close, but how do you handle men with firearms?" asked Sergeant Fenwick as he removed his Colt .45 and held it, barrel facing the ceiling. "The hills are filled with men with firearms and hot tempers. We've even had a few shootouts here in town, at the saloons and even duels in the street. Old Betsey here is my best protection when the lead starts flying around," said Sergeant Fenwick as he caressed the barrel of his .45 and then holstered it.

"There's no getting around it, Jim. Some situations will absolutely require firearms. My intention is to reduce their use to a minimum by not resorting to their use. If a man comes to Juneau, and wants to shoot up the place, we're going to discourage it. To fire back will just fall into his wishes and lead will be flying around increasing the chance that someone is gonna get hurt. I know this all sounds kind of silly to you all, but we're gonna give it a try. Huang is bringing a man from San Francisco with him. He's a teacher, a man who has studied Wing Chung Kung Fu for many years. He'll be teaching me and my deputies the secrets of the Orient and ways to counteract even firearms.

"Now since I've got you all here, I know you're involved. We're gonna make Juneau a better place. Unleash your creative talents and bring a new spirit to Juneau, We need schools and hospitals, theater and culture. The people have the answers within them.

There is so much talent out there..."

Suddenly the door flew open and Billy Hendricks, a shopkeeper's boy ran up to Johnny, "Sheriff Brady, Soapy Smith and his men are over in the Water Inn. There's been some trouble and a few of his men are wrecking the place. The house manager sent me over to get ya; he says he needs ya right away."

"Well things are heating up already. I thought Soapy was still in Pine Log. The talkin' stops now, I gotta earn my keep. Sergeant Fenwick, I could use you as a backup man. Stay outta sight, if the lead starts flying I'll need you. As I was saying, we all got a job to do and I'd appreciate it if you could hold up your end. We'll meet here same time tomorrow. Thanks for coming." Johnny took a drink from a water glass and headed for the door.

"Thanks, Willie, just stay outta sight." Johnny headed for the Water Inn Hole. There was a full moon and a chill in the air. He could hear a ruckus going on in the brightly lit saloon. There were about ten horses hitched to a post just outside the saloon. Johnny knew they belonged to Soapy and his gang. Steam emanated from their nostrils as if they'd just ridden hard into town.

They haven't been there too long and they're already starting trouble. Johnny took out the sheriff's badge and pinned it on his leather jacket. He peered into a side window. He could see two men intimidating players standing up near the table. One took a chair and crashed it against a mirror near a stairwell used to gain entrance to the rented rooms above the saloon; seated at the bar, with his head down and several cronies nearby, was the notorious Soapy Smith. Johnny could identify him by his long, flowing, salt and pepper beard. The men at the bar seemed oblivious to the commotion in the back of the saloon. Johnny could account for seven of the men and wondered where the other three might be.

He entered the saloon through the swinging doors. All eyes in the place focused on the newly appointed sheriff. A man who had just overturned a table caught a glance at his fixated audience and turned to see who had taken the attention away from himself.

"I'd appreciate it if you would take it easy on the furniture young fella, cause it belongs to a friend of mine," said Johnny in a low key voice, as if he'd just come upon an accident.

"Well, what do ya know? The Black Irishman sheriff is here. Been wanting to meet the man who's gonna stop me from having my fun in town." Several men standing near the card table moved to the side of the room sensing a confrontation. Those seated near Soapy Smith got up from their stools and readied themselves for action. Soapy stayed seated, glued to his drink, and just turned his head momentarily as if distracted by a fly. "That mirror you accidentally broke cost a pretty penny. Miss Brown told me it just arrived from San Francisco last week."

"'Twas no accident, you mick; I intentionally broke it like I'm thinking a breaking something on your face," said the well-muscled man with a scraggy beard and wearing a beaver skin vest "'Twas no accident at all, Mr. sheriff. We always like to meet with the law in every town we visit. Kind of put them in their place. Ya know, let them know where they stand. You could say I was trying to flush you out to see what you're made of. Right boys!" He turned in the direction of Soapy Smith who still had his head down, nursing his drink.

Johnny walked over to the broken mirror. The men stiffened their bodies, readying themselves for action as Johnny walked between them, bent down, and picked up a shard of glass about the size of a plate, and looked at the wreckage at his feet. "I'd say this mirror cost Miss Brown over sixty dollars wouldn't you?" he asked.

"Yea, I'd say just about sixty dollars she's out," said the man in the beaver skin vest as he watched Johnny's every move, his face growing more sinister, annoyed at this placating, talkative lawman.

"You know it's going to have to be replaced," said Johnny as he righted the overturned table.

"And who's gonna have to replace it, sheriff?"

The men behind the beaver vested man and Johnny made a commotion as they moved out of the line of fire as they sensed the talking was coming to an end. Johnny walked closer to the man and looked him in the eye. "Them that broke it," he said slowly. All his senses were keyed up as he waited for the reply.

"What do you think we should pay them with, Dahmer?

"How bout with some lead!"

Johnny saw the man to his side reaching for his gun. He immediately fired the shard of glass at his arm as he was withdrawing the gun from his holster. The man let out a scream. The man in front of him took a step back and reached for his gun. Johnny moved in fast, slapped the gun to this side and followed with three quick blows: one to his midriff and two to his face and jaw. The gun went off and clattered to the floor as the man fell unconscious to his knees, then pitched forward unaware of what had struck him. Those gathered in the saloon were amazed at the speed of the events. Several of Soapy Smith's men reached for their guns belatedly. Johnny got behind the man holding his bleeding arm and used him for cover.

Sergeant Fenwick burst into the saloon with a shotgun in hand. "Don't!" he yelled as Soapy Smith's men realized a Mountie was holding them at bay, the queen's lawmen were quite respected even by Soapy's men and they thought better of having a run in with the Crown.

Johnny helped the man in a beaver-skin vest to his feet. He sat him in a chair. The other man with the bleeding arm was helped to a chair also. Johnny cut away his shirt and stemmed the flow of blood with strips of tablecloth.

Suddenly three men burst into the saloon, they wrested the shotgun away from Sergeant Fenwick and one pounded him on the head with the butt of his gun. Fenwick fell to the floor. Soapy's men rushed Johnny. He dispatched one with a quick kick and another with two blows to the head, but three attacked at once and toppled him over, and they wrestled him to the ground. An explosion stopped the fighting. Johnny looked up and there was Soapy holding a smoking gun aimed at his head.

"I oughta blow your brains out here and now. I've done it before many times. You think your fancy footwork can stop this." He thrust the gun under Johnny's nose. He cocked the gun and was about to fire when a lookout yelled to him.

"Soapy, there's a crowd gathering at the sheriff's office. I think they are headed this way! They look agitated."

Soapy uncocked the gun. "Let this be a warning, sheriff," he spat on the floor with contempt at the word *sheriff*. 'The next time I come into town, I better not be bothered with the likes of you. Do your paperwork and stay out of sight. You're a lucky man, you are not dead. I'm giving you your life back. Now who owns this town? Answer me!"

"You do, for now"

"Why you idiot; you're a slow learner!" He planted a kick to Johnny's stomach and grabbed a chair and broke it over Johnny's head.

Johnny went unconscious. Soapy looked around the saloon with an intimidating grin. He walked over to Sergeant Fenwick who was still out from the blow to his head. "I told you guys to go easy on the Crown. Now you'll be drawing the Mounties from Canada into Juneau and we will have to stay out of sight for a while till they withdraw. Let's go! Grab a few bottles of that good whiskey and bring it along with you. And now my good friends," he spread his hand in an expansive gesture as if pleading with his audience, "who owns this town?"

"You do, Soapy" said the audience in a staccato of utterances as Soapy's glance surveyed the crowd looking for a dissenter, His baleful glare fell upon Willie Annue who had slipped into the saloon unnoticed in an attempt to help Johnny, but the ensuing events made him fear for his life.

"You do, Mr. Smith!" said Willie, "Lock, stock and barrel!"

"Now that's better, the next time I come to town I expect to receive a warmer welcome. Pass the word to Mayor Biggs that I expect him to have the income tax and the sewerage tax and the prospector's fee paid in gold. I'll be bringing in several wagons and we'll be holding the city revenues until I can have my own bank built. Tell that fatheaded windbag, Mayor Biggs that I expect full compliance with my wishes. I'll be giving him fifteen days warning before I make my collection. Why there are roads to be built, and hospitals and schools be constructed." He looked at his men, some of whom were talking to the girls who worked the saloon. "Let's go, men! Leave them purty young ladies alone. There are enough orphans running around town we don't want to create any more." Soapy chuckled to himself as he departed the Water Inn followed by his entourage.

Ten minutes later a crowd of citizens entered the saloon with guns drawn. Johnny and Sergeant Fenwick were seated at a table and were nursing their head wounds. Margie Upak looked at Johnny and started to wipe the blood that matted his hair.

"Guess we have to train harder. Margie, tell Huang I'd like to see him, right away! And to bring that fellow, Dave Fresney, the Wing Chung man.

# CHAPTER XVI

D ave Fresney, son of a British sea captain who commanded an English freighter out of Singapore dismissed the class of police recruits. His job in training the 180 man San Francisco Police Department was nearing its completion. Eight weeks ago these men had been well intentioned young men seeking a career in law enforcement. Whatever the good intentions that had motivated them to join the department, these unfit cadets were no match for the wild, devil-may-care, low-life criminal elements who were turning San Francisco into the most crime-ridden city in America.

Dave had been summoned from Scotland Yard where he held the position of Physical Director and Martial Arts Training Instructor. He jumped at the opportunity to work in the wild, Wild West of the States. His mother was an American, born in Brooklyn, New York so he wanted to learn about the country of her birth. He saw a golden opportunity to introduce Wing Clung and many of the other martial arts he had learned in China and Japan. He possessed three black belts of the highest degree. His father's tenure in China enabled him to receive the finest in instruction in the martial arts. Training in Kendo, Karate and Wing Chung Kung Fu was given to him by masters in exchange for free passage to any port in Europe. David had listened well and endured all kinds of privation, injury and insults during his apprentice in the martial arts. At the age of twenty he was the most renowned teacher in England. His skill was respected and surpassed by only a handful of teachers on mainland China and Japan. When his father returned to

England, David was in great demand both as a teacher/instructor and as a stoic philosopher of the wisdom of Kung Fu.

He had trained thousands of young Britons in the art of self-defense. The mention of David's name brought bows of deference from the legion of black belts he had trained and certified. He had single-handedly popularized Kung Fu in Europe. Now, after twenty years of teaching law enforcement officers, he longed to travel to North America and visit the country of his mother's birth. Jenny Carpenter had fallen in love with the handsome British seaman when her father had invited him over to meet his children. The seventeen year old Irish girl fell in love at first sight with the boyish looking twenty-two year old English seaman. Their whirlwind marriage in New York and immediate return to England had filled a void in Harold Fresney's life. He steadily moved up the ranks and received the captaincy of his own ship just five years after marrying Jenny. One year after David's birth he was assigned to captain a huge British freighter based in Singapore.

When David was eight years old his father took him along on a month long stay to the port of Heinen in Japan. Their cargo of cedar and hardwoods from Canada lent a pungent fragrance to the sea air as the freighter approached the Japanese archipelago. The young boy was flushed with excitement as the freighter neared the port city of Heinen. The first extended trip with his father familiarized the boy to faces and personalities heard over dinner discussions in the family household. He saw how the men respected his father and the great responsibilities involved in captaining a British freighter loaded with much needed cargo. An earthquake and fire had destroyed a portion of the city of Heinen six months earlier.

David and his father were housed in the outskirts of Heinen in a small cottage near a Shinto temple. The cottage was sparsely furnished with tatami mats neatly positioned in each room. A servant girl of eighteen cooked their meals and answered their questions about daily living. David grew to admire the beauty and grace of their hostess in the performance of even the simplest household chore. Her shy laughter at David's attempts at humor made him instinctively like her very much.

One day, when David's father had been called to the city to supervise the loading of his ship, David wandered into the grounds of the Shinto temple. He was drawn to the beauty of the manicured garden and the winding garden path that led to a wooden bridge leading into the temple area. As he neared the apex of the oval bridge he bent down and picked up pebbles to drop in the water below. Ripples powered outward toward the moss covered rocks. Multi-colored goldfish rose to the surface and lapped up the thrown pebbles only to spit them out as they descended. A clacking sound soon broke his reveries. It was the sound of wood being slapped against wood. Suddenly it stopped. A few short seconds later it resumed. This time he could hear audible grunts. He dumped his handful of pebbles and moved toward the temple cautiously, not sure he was welcome.

The smell of incense wafted out from the door that was held only slightly ajar. Inside a crowd of uniformly dressed men were engrossed in a demonstration taking place in the center of the temple. The clacking of wood resumed and a cloud of dust arose over the heads of the spectators. David slipped into the temple unnoticed and moved to his right where an opening would allow a better view.

Two men with wooden sticks were facing each other. Their faces ware covered with sweat and their gaze never left the other's face. They stalked each other in catlike movements, eyes locked unto each other's every motion. Each circled the other until one raced forward to land a crashing blow. In an instant the intended victim moved but inches, the wooden bokken landed embedded in the dust of the arena. The aggressor attempted to raise the bokken but a slashing blow to his neck ended the combat. Both combatants bowed to each other and walked toward their respective handlers; the winner congratulated, the loser consoled. The clacking of wood resumed and two warriors again faced each other, bokken in hand. A monk robed in black held a bell. The two warriors bowed to each other. At the sound of the bell they raised their wooden bokkens and stalked each other. Circling each other they looked intently for a lapse of concentration that would signal an opening for attack. Beads of sweat grew on their brows. The dust kicked up by their sandaled feet mixed with the sweat and gave their faces a savage visage.

David stared in heightened anxiety waiting for the coming attack. The men circled each other; one man raised his bokken, the other waited for the imminent attack. Nothing happened. They reversed their stalking, now going counter clockwise. Their eyes locked unto each other's motion. Five, then ten minutes passed. Neither had struck, yet tension filled the air. David knew he was witnessing something special but he couldn't define it. Nothing had yet taken place. He had never experienced it before yet he knew a great battle was taking place. It was all in the mind of the combatants. The beads of sweat, mixed with the fine dust. A ferocity held in check by mutual admiration for the defensive skills of each warrior finally relented as the bell sounded again. They bowed to each other, the assembled audience clapped in enthusiasm confirming David's analysis of the bout.

"It was a good fight wasn't it, child?" said a short powerfully built man in a monk's robe. A solid, muscled jaw lined his oriental features. "Though not a blow was struck, a great battle was taking place. Every maneuver of one was read by the other. We call this mind boxing. Each of those men is a champion in his own province. Neither decided to land a blow because to do so would have caused defeat to one, and renown to the other. It was a battle worth pondering over and many lessons were internalized by the audience. The martial arts teach that restraint in battle is just as important as aggressiveness. The enemy must be measured because life is so precious. What is your name child?"

"David."

"I am Funokoshi, Director of Physical Training here at the temple. Perhaps you would like to know more about the martial arts. It is an unending journey and your character will be tested and strengthened. I have a class here for young people every night."

"I would have to ask my father. He is the captain of a freighter and we live nearby. How much will it cost?"

"Tell your father I would like to speak to him. Do not worry about the cost. Your unexpected entry into our temple on the Day of the Lion tells me a warrior in a child's clothing seeks instruction. Things will be worked out. Come with your father this evening at seven p.m. You will meet the other students.'

"Thank you, sir, I mean Mr. Funokoshi."

The rhythmic clacking sound of sticks announced the beginning of another match. This time two ferocious looking Samurai warriors clad in armor entered the arena. David looked on in fascination as the two men bowed to each other and prepared for battle, their assistants adjusting protective head gear. Funokoshi turned toward David. "You must leave now. The use of the Samurai sword is not to be revealed to strangers until a long apprenticeship has taken place. He walked David to the temple doors. They passed through a manicured garden leading to the footbridge. David could hear the metallic sound of steel reverberating from the arena and wondered what was taking place. A yearning to know more about the world of the Samurai had taken root in his heart

"I will be here with my father tonight Mr. Funokoshi." He bowed to the powerfully built man as he had seen others do and looked forward to beginning the journey of the Samurai warrior.

"You are to be commended for taking advantage of your stay in Japan by learning the martial arts. For the code of the Samurai will give you strength for life's journey." The sound of applause emanated from the arena and David imagined himself the victorious warrior.

# CHAPTER XV

These were the defenders of Juneau, a motley crew if there ever was one; Johnny looked around and saw his true friends. He asked for volunteers to go into training for the coming battle against Soapy and his brigands. Only five men volunteered their services. The rest pleaded hardship, what with families to care for or claims to be mined. These men: Chuck Harris, the blacksmith; Kyoto, the cook; Willie Annue, the Eskimo; Sergeant Fenwick; and old man Huang, the tailor stood up and sided with Johnny. Johnny tried to talk Huang out of volunteering but the old tailor wouldn't back down. His journey with David Fresney to the Juneau had brought out his hidden martial spirit and now his friend Johnny was in dire trouble. "I am on old man; my children are grown and have families of their own. Order is the first law of the universe. This is my hometown and my friends have been threatened. I stay!"

There was a knock at the door. Johnny opened it and the smiling, bearded face of Jack Schwartz beamed at him. "Thought you could use a little help, Johnny. I tried to bring a couple of my friends along but when they heard Soapy was the problem, they thought better of it. Some of the men are still cleaning up broken windows from last week's visit. Seems Soapy's men like to grab whatever strikes their fancy from the store windows on Main Street. I'm a bit tired of it and when I heard you could use a few good men...well, what can I do?"

Big Jack Schwartz stood six feet four inches in his stocking feet. He owned a hardware store on Main Street, had spurred the building of the community's first synagogue, and was active in all kinds of community organizations. "Jack, you're a welcomed addition. You know Chuck Harris, this is Willie Annue, Kyoto, from Margie's place, Huang, the tailor, Sergeant Fenwick and this here is Dave Fresney; he's going train us in the martial arts."

Jack shook hands all around. "I heard about Dave when I was in San Francisco last month. People feel safe walking the streets again. You've become a legend in Frisco. Daytime shootouts and bank robberies are now ancient history. The merchants gave Dave quite a going away party. Business is now booming. You know Soapy used to be active down that way, but the heat got too intense so he decided to go up north with his brigade. When I heard Dave was in town I had to come and join you Johnny, to see the man up close. It's about time we stopped Soapy and his friends. The merchants are tired of paying tribute to him."

"Well men, I understand we have three weeks to prepare for Soapy's next arrival. That means we have to train intensively. Plan on spending the day. You all are gonna feel mighty sore for a while. You're going to be using muscles you never knew you had. The first week will be dedicated to learning the art of Wing Chung Kung Fu; the second week, Karate; and the third week, Kendo. We will be constantly talking about the art of warfare and strategy. You will be alert as you never have been before and you will be able to face combat in a calm, prepared and natural state. Usually I have at least several months to train police cadets, but under the circumstances we face, we've got to learn and be ready for battle in three weeks. Are you up for the challenge? It's not going to be easy, but you are embarking on a journey that will make you better men. It will also save your life. You're going to be taking a crash course in what it means to be a Samurai, a fighting man. Half the battle is won because you have volunteered. Volunteers make the best soldiers because they are motivated. The first thing we're going to work on is balance. Without proper balance in your stance..."

Johnny felt the stirring in his mind of something deep and long forgotten. It was the martial spirit. The spirit of his adopted father, Harold Green, a Civil War veteran came to mind. The Judge had been a great warrior. David was a small man with the heart of a warrior. In repose: calm, natural, easily approachable; in battle: lightening quick, precise and always thinking. His movements were the result of thousands of hours of practice in real and simulated combat.

"We will be breaking down the movements into katas. Katas are techniques that we'll be practicing over and over again. Every time you perform a kata correctly you are casting a pebble into the stream of perfect technique. Performed over time, a bridge will form in the unconscious and all your actions will be deliberate; in perfect response to the threat one experiences," said David as he deflected a blow from Sergeant Fenwick and, in an instant, dealt what could have been a lightning fast crushing response. The men paired off and practiced the simple technique over and over again.

"We'll be performing Velum Tao daily; Celum Tao is approximately fifteen separate movements that over time blend into each other. We will be learning three sections of Celum Tao. At first the movements will seem strange. As time goes by, you will see how everything relates to these movements. Learn Celum Tao and all your movements will be more fluid and natural," said David.

The men formed a semi-circle with David demonstrating the movements of Velum Tao. Later Johnny paired with big Jack Schwartz and practiced blocks and parries. Then they watched as David demonstrated counter strikes to the blocks and parries. It was the speed of the strikes that mesmerized Johnny.

After several hours the men rested and talked. Water and light snacks were available. The men talked animatedly about what had occurred and Johnny could tell that a long dormant something was freed within them. It was as if a tiger within them had been freed for a while and they felt better because of it.

# CHAPTER XVI

Sue laid back on the couch grateful the swelling in her leg had subsided. Whatever wonders Doc had performed to save her leg were working beautifully. The ugly red streaks had disappeared and feeling was returning to the injured leg. She raised her head and fluffed up the pillow and then settled back. She looked around the warm, cozy room and was grateful for being alive. She thought of Johnny.

A gentle knocking on the door woke her from her reveries. "Come in, the door's open."

Johnny walked over to her and gently kissed her lips. She embraced him and they kissed and hungered for each other, trading long sensuous kisses. She moaned under his caresses. "Damned leg, I can't wait until it heals. Doc says it'll be a couple of weeks before I can get around. I missed you so, Johnny. I heard about the run-in with Soapy and his gang. Johnny, we can leave Juneau, I love you so I don't want to see you get hurt. I've got more money than we could ever need." She pulled him down and they traded mad, loving kisses.

"We're staying right here. I'm not gonna let a bandit like Soapy chase us out of Juneau. What could we say to our kids, when we have them," he looked into her eyes which were wide with surprise and agreement. "There was trouble and we left. No, if we ever leave Juneau, it'll be because there are greater opportunities elsewhere, for us or for our kids." Sue's eyes watered and she drew him down to the couch where they embraced and fondled each other.

A rooster crowed in the hen house not far from the main house. Johnny got up and dressed. He splashed cold water on his face from a basin near the bed. He rubbed the fine bristle on his face thinking he'd have to save the shave for when he got home. Sunlight cascaded into the room announcing the start of a beautiful day. The cold, howling winds and snows had subsided. Johnny got up and looked down at the woman who had changed his life forever. Her full hips gave a lovely curvature to the silk sheet covering her body. The dawn light cascading into the large bedroom filled the room with sunshine. Johnny felt that he could move the world for this woman, fight any foe or create beauty in his art as he had never done before. He must paint a picture of Sue, he told himself.

He went to the kitchen and made coffee. The crowing rooster reminded him there must be eggs around. He walked through the foot deep snow into the hen house and returned with several eggs. He threw several logs into the wood burning stove. The roaring fire edged out the morning chill and the smell of bacon and eggs made him feel he could love the domestic life. Drinking slowly from a steaming mug of hot coffee, he savored this sweet moment in time. Now I have everything I've always wanted. It was love that had been missing from his life; the love of a man for a woman. He poured a cup of coffee and placed it on a tray with the bacon and eggs. He finished off the remaining eggs and bacon, and brought the tray into Sue's room. Placing it on a night table, he bent down and gently massaged her face with flickering kisses. She awoke from her slumber, saw him and placed both hands on his face and drew him close for a long sensuous kiss.

"Sue, we gonna have to get married and soon. Will you marry me? Soon? I don't think I can stand being away from you. I hate to leave you. Last night you filled me with a joy that I've never known was possible. And at my age, I just about thought I knew most things. I feel like twenty years old again. Like I just about can accomplish anything I set my mind to. Being with you makes me feel anything is possible. I'm in love, Sue. What are we going to do about it?"

"We're going to get married, Johnny. Father Mike was always telling me that something was missing in my life and now I feel complete. Here we, two people who held off doing the most natural of things because we were so hard to please. Not anymore! We're going to have a church wedding as soon as possible. The biggest wedding Juneau has seen in a long time! I love you, Johnny. We're starting late, but I want to have kids as soon as possible; lots of them if God will let us. Oh. That's right, you're not a Catholic?"

"Sue, I am now. I've been interested in the catholic religion for a long time. Hell, I'd become a Zen Buddhist for you, sweetheart! They embraced and kissed. "Hey, you better eat your bacon and eggs before they get cold. I'm going back into town. The Kung Fu lessons are ending today. Tomorrow, Kyoto, the cook at Margie Upak's place will be giving us lessons in Karate. We're starting to meld together as a fighting force. There are only seven of us against Soapy's thirty to forty men, but I wouldn't want to be with a better bunch of guys. When Soapy and his brigands come to town to collect the taxes, he'll be up against a fighting force with right and might on its side. Dave's constantly talking strategy, teaching us to think differently. He's a genius in the art of being a warrior,"

"Johnny, bullets can kill anybody, no matter how good a fighter they are,"

"I know, Sue. Dave's working on a scheme to disarm them. He figures most of the men with Soapy are just

89

down on their luck; disgruntled prospectors and ner-do-wells with a penchant for violence. He aims to give them a good drubbing and a chance to change their ways. The real killers and psychopaths are going to have to be treated differently. That's the tough part, the dangerous part. Only training and constant repetition of katas can prepare us to deal with this problem. The training is working. I can't describe how I've changed in just two weeks. I'm more alive, more sure of myself, more assertive and yet I have a great abhorrence for violence of any kind. Somewhere inside of Soapy Smith he killed off the better angels of his nature and he's trying to make his men the same way. Misery loves company and he's doing his damnedest to make a world for his men that leaves no room for compromise and civility. Only brute force matters. That's why we need Dave. He's dealt with the worst in human nature and has come out of it with his integrity and principles still intact. His moral base has been strengthened with each encounter with evil. He radiates a goodness that has grown out of contact with unprincipled, violent men. We are learning in three weeks the wisdom of a lifetime of disciplined reactions. And it comes from the Orient. I have great admiration for a people who have perfected the skills of a warrior."

"There's a history of barbarity and cruelty that comes from the Orient, too," said Sue, as she recalled being told that baby girls are sometimes drowned because they are thought of little value in a society that preferred male workers over females. Sue had fought this macho ethic all her life.

"There's plenty of barbarity and cruelty in every nation. Just walk the streets of Juneau, we have our street urchins and alcoholics and public duels over words muttered in a saloon or a dispute at cards. We have much to learn from the Orient, I never realized it before, but I'm leaning..."

"Johnny, are you there?"

The pounding on the downstairs door sent Johnny scurrying down the stairs. Something's wrong in town, thought Johnny as he unlatched the bolt.

It was Scratchy Wilson, a regular at the Water Inn Hole. "Johnny, they done burn the place down. Escaped with my life, I did! Poured kerosene over the whole place and laughed as they lit the match."

"What did they burn down, Scratchy? Who did it?"

"A couple of Soapy's men came into town; they were roaring drunk and somebody let out how we were training to fight them on Tax Day. I tried to shush him but he just went on and on. Now Soapy's gonna know about it," said Scratchy itching himself all over, a habit that got more pronounced as anxiety increased. "A few other stores caught fire, they still trying to put them out..."

"Wait here. I'll be right with you and stop that damn itching, Scratchy, it's habit forming," said Johnny as he raced upstairs to tell Sue. He found himself brushing off his shirt sleeves on the way up.

# CHAPTER XVII

J ohnny stood and watched as the last dying ember that had once been the Water Inn Hole was doused by the Juneau Fire Brigade. Several stores nearby had been torched. Reggie Jones, a longtime proprietor of a general store walked over to Johnny, both hands clutched the sides of his head. "Crazy people! My life was in that store. Never had an enemy; now this. We should have never threatened to go up against these people. Just give 'em what they want. The mad man was laughing. Had people been in the store they could have been hurt!"

"I'm sorry, Reggie. I didn't know people could be so rotten. We'll call a meeting and see if we can't rebuild. I'm going to have to go after them, Reggie. No use waiting for the next attack. Soapy needs a lesson, and a whipping. I'll bring him to justice, Reggie. I'll find the men who did this and lock them up. Sue Brown lost a lot, too, Reggie."

"Look out, Johnny!" screamed Reggie, as he ran away from Johnny.

Johnny turned to see three riders bearing down on him. The slush from the city street shot high above the racing hooves of the horses. One of the men took aim with a rifle, Johnny reflexively moved to his left as a shot bored into the ground several feet behind him. The rider with the rifle moved ahead of the two other pistol bearing riders. Johnny was glad he did. He now had a shield he had to use or he was a goner. The rifleman was now only thirty five feet away taking dead aim from the speeding horse. Johnny waited an instant to make sure all the rifleman's concentration was focused on that shot. Suddenly he raced forward toward the rifleman.

That move so disoriented the rifleman, he lowered the rifle. He couldn't believe a man, standing weaponless, would charge a rifleman and his horse. He had only fifteen feet now to dislodge a shot at the crazy man charging him. He raised the rifle again, but it was too late. A leaping hand grabbed the barrel while another grabbed the back of his vest He was hoisted completely clear of the saddle and landed face first in the muck and black embers of the Juneau city street. Weaponless, he tried to clear his eyes of the muck and slush. What he saw next, he would never forget.

His friends pulled up short with their horses and were about to shoot him thinking he was Johnny. Suddenly, at an angle, a riderless horse came at a fury toward them. Realizing what had happened, the pistol bearing men waited for Johnny to get upright for a clean shot. Instead, the horse raced at them. Fearing for their lives, they took aim at the horse and shot. Two bullets in the head brought the horse to a crashing fall into the muck.

Johnny struggled to get the horse between him and the men. Shots rang out repeatedly. Warm blood splattered Johnny's face, but he was unhurt; except for the anger he felt at losing such a life-saving horse like this one. He patted the horse even as bullets pounded into the horses flesh and the horse abruptly fell lifeless. Johnny waited until both men had emptied their pistols. Then he rose from behind the horse, rifle in hand. The men looked as if they had seen an apparition. They backed up until they bumped into the rifleman who had been on the horse. They raised their hands in surrender and pleaded for mercy. "Don't shoot! Please Mr. Brady! Soapy made us do it! He told us to put the fear of God in you, he did! He said you'd run scared like all the rest. We had to do it."

"You killed a fine horse there; he saved my life. You burned down half a city block and stole the livelihood from some wonderful people. You tried to ambush me and now you plead for mercy. I feel like killing all three of you, right here, right now. But that would be too good for you guys. You're gonna serve time and the people of Juneau will determine how long. You'll receive something from them that you never gave to others, a fair chance. And, maybe through all of this, it had to come to this," Johnny slowly pointed to the burned wreckage about him and the dead horse lying in the street. "Maybe then you'll have learned something about living in harmony with your fellow man. You're still alive and where there's life there's hope, but I doubt it with you guys," Johnny spat into the street. "But before I stick you in jail, we're gonna bury that fine horse. What was his name?"

"Lightening," said the rifleman, his head bowed in remorse. "He was a good horse."

"I know it," said Johnny. "He saved my life, Reggie. Get me a few shovels. These three men are gonna move that horse to the top of the hill where the animal cemetery is.

"Let's get to it!"

The three men stared in disbelief as they looked toward the animal cemetery, more than a mile away.

# CHAPTER XVIII

They buried the horse. Johnny went home and told Sue about the Inn and the surrounding damage. They sat down and talked a long while about what had happened. Sue talked about her love for the Water Inn Hole. It was the first of her many investments in Juneau. She had turned a run-down old saloon into a first rate eating and dining establishment. On opening day, the prospectors timidly walked in with their hats in hand, afraid to get dirt on the new carpeting. The gambling tables were topped with lush green felt and the food was delicious. Sue made the girls who wanted to work in her place wear the latest fashions from San Francisco. She hired a bartender who used to be a Pinkerton detective to keep a semblance of order in the establishment. Within six months, the Water Inn Hole was *the place* in town for food and drink and a little fun.

From the profit on the Water Inn Hole she began to invest in building modest hotels for the prospectors who struck it rich and wanted a decent home to display their wealth and for out-of-town salesmen who looked with disdain on the tent city that was Juneau in the early days. The hotels were filled within days of opening. She began to build grander, more opulent hotels with their own casinos and fine dining. She hired professional hotel management people from New York to handle her burgeoning financial empire. She consulted with them daily and okayed all major purchases.

"We're just going to have to rebuild, Johnny. A while back, a wise man was passing through Juneau on his way to San Francisco. He tried to sell insurance to the prospectors who had struck it rich in the field. They all laughed in his face, but the more he talked, the more sense it made. This isn't my first loss Johnny. I've had other losses. One time, if you remember, we had that major landslide from weeks of heavy rain. One of my hotels was buried under tons of debris. It was scheduled for opening in just two weeks. Disaster struck but, thanks to that insurance man, I was able to rebuild within a year. The new hotel has a restaurant called the Down Under, a private joke."

"You mean you got insurance on the Inn?" asked Johnny.

"On the Inn and the whole block, Johnny. Those stores paid rent for the land they sit on. I told them when they first got established they would be paying a higher rent than usual, but that someday they wouldn't regret it. I guess that day is today. We'll be able to rebuild within weeks. I sent a telegram to our man in San Francisco. He's coming here pronto to survey the damage."

"Well, there's going to be some mighty happy shopkeepers when they hear the good news," said Johnny, touching the brim of his hat out of respect for Sue's foresight and intelligence. "When Soapy Smith hears about what happened to his henchmen, he ain't gonna be too happy. I'm hoping the loss of three of his men will make him think a little, but I doubt it. Dave says we need more training, that we have to work on a strategy that will divide and conquer his forces. If he gives us the time to prepare for his entry into Juneau we can take him and his men. If he comes in the next day or so we'll have a big problem on our hands."

"Would it help to call in some Pinkertons from San Francisco? They helped out in the riots and during the great fire. I have in my employ a man who could get in contact with the president of that company. We could have a number of them here in several weeks," said Sue.

"Well it's an option, but it's too costly. It's best for the town to solve its own problems." Johnny reached across the table and held Sue's hand. Their fingers intertwined.

"What about us, Johnny? What does the future hold for us?"

"I've been thinking about that. Would you marry me, Sue? Say after this mess with Soapy Smith is cleaned up.

"Of course, Johnny," she leaned forward and planted a kiss on his lips.

"I gotta go now, Sue. Dave's working on a strategy to divide and conquer Soapy's forces. He figures a raid on Soapy's encampment may provoke Soapy into sending a few more men after us. There's a danger he could overreact and bring his whole gang into Juneau. That would spell trouble."

When Johnny arrived in Juneau he went to the Knights Hall where Kyoto was teaching Karate to the men. "The form of Karate I teach is called Goju-Ryu. It combines Kung Fu and Karate. In Japanese, *go* means *hard* or *strong*, and *ju* means *soft* or *gentle*. The word *ryu* means *style*. The term *goju* comes from a line in an ancient Chinese poem: 'Everything in the universe is breathing hard and soft.' I believe that to be happy or successful in life, a person has to know when to stand up against another and when to give in; when to talk and when to listen; when to act and when to wait. It is important to know when to fight, but it is more important to know when not to fight."

"We will begin this class with a brief period of meditation. Meditation will clear your mind and you will put aside other distractions and focus upon learning

Karate. As we close our eyes and meditate you will learn relaxation, patience and self-control," said Kyoto.

After meditation he led the men into a series of warm-up stretching exercises. They worked on proper balance, strikes, parries, blocks and kicks. Kyoto talked all the while, imbuing in them a different way of thinking. "This all seems foreign now, but if we constantly practice, one day a bridge of bodily understanding will take place. Like pebbles dropped in a stream, after a while enough are there to make a crossing." He talked of war strategy and shared tales of incredible courage from the Orient. They took a break for lunch then resumed practice with weapons.

Kyoto demonstrated defenses against attackers with knives, sticks and clubs. "There is an instant, if only for a mini-second, when the attacker will have a slight lapse of concentration. An instant when his eyes are elsewhere or he takes a long breath. It is then you must enter heaven and counter attack."

He called Johnny forward. He raised his long stick as if to strike Johnny. "You see hell is out there where the main part of the club will land a crushing blow. Heaven is penetrating inside toward the handle and counter attacking. It is the same with a sword or club. Toward the handle there is safety. Out there is death or hell. In your own lives you can learn a lesson. When one is involved, say, in your work world, you are able to understand everything that is going on. When you are not involved or inside, your enemy can plot your demise. Stay involved at the center of things, so you will know what is taking place."

The group took turns to find lapses in Kyoto's defenses. A few succeeded in entering heaven. They began to become aware of their surroundings in a way they had never experienced. Kyoto was pleased with their first lesson. "You have started on a long journey; the study of the martial arts will reward you immensely. The confidence you gain will make you a better person."

"What if I kill someone using the techniques you have taught us? They seem very deadly." asked Annue.

"It is better to be judged by twelve than to be carried by six," replied Kyoto.

The men nodded in agreement.

# CHAPTER XIX

Tony Mendez, a Filipino grocer decided to respond to Johnny's request for help. Juneau had been good to him and his family. While men hungered after gold, Tony knew he could make gold filling their bodily hunger. He moved his family to Juneau but not before making contact with suppliers for rice, coffee, fruit, yams, herbal teas, dried fruit and other grocery products. They would be shipped on a weekly basis from suppliers in San Francisco. Within a year he was supplying the major hotels with foodstuff and doing a brisk business at his grocery store.

Tony was 5'1" in height and weighed less than 120 pounds, but he knew the Filipino martial art of Kali. He walked to the center of the room carrying only two bamboo sticks less than three feet long. "Gentlemen, when I heard you needed a few good men to stand up to Soapy and his gang, I felt a need to share with you the ancient art of Kali; some know it as stick fighting. It is an extremely effective martial art when performed properly. It is an ancient art. We start with an innocuous looking stick approximately two and a half feet in length. It is made of bamboo or rattan. It has a very strong quality to it. It will not shatter or break. When wielding our stick we grasp it three inches above the end of the stick. This leaves a three inch protrusion that we will use for trapping and blocking our opponents thrust. We wield the stick in a pattern. Follow me!" Tony slashed a short $X$ near the upper torso and then proceeded to make a longer $X$ from the toes past the shoulder. Two short chops at the knee-caps, across the midsection and a thrust at the belly.

"The return stroke mirrors the slash at every point. You must practice for hours to integrate the strokes into your being. We will now put down the sticks to work on coordinating our strokes." He had the men pair off and practice open palm strikes against each other. "You must develop a sensitivity to your opponent's rhythm; by mirroring your opponent's actions your sensitivity improves. Now pick up your sticks and resume the pattern I have taught you," said Tony as he observed the students. The rhythmic clacking of sticks reverberated about the room. Tony walked among the men correcting their stroking.

"Now we will practice trapping our opponents stick and dealing counter blows to disable them." He had Johnny wield his stick in a slashing motion. Tony countered with a block, slid his stick down toward his opponent's wrist and used the three inch protrusion to trap and pressure the wrist until Johnny dropped his stick. Tony taught the class locks, blocks and blows. This little piece of rattan became a powerful weapon when wielded by a skillful practitioner. The men spent the whole afternoon learning the art of Kali.

Johnny shared his enthusiasm about stick fighting with Sue; she listened with interest and when he had finished, she said, "Johnny, I have something to tell you. You know that boarding house I had on the edge of town, The Crystal Lodge. I've turned it into a home for homeless children. You wouldn't believe how happy the children are. We already have sixty-five kids. The girls are on the second floor, the boys occupy the first floor. The third floor is going to be a school where the kids will learn trades besides learning reading, writing and math. I'm so excited, I feel so good about it. This morning I found volunteers willing to help out. We're going to create a Board of Trustees who'll oversee the home. We went right through the streets of Juneau and roused the kids from their wooden crates, from the sidewalks and back alleys, and took them all down to The Crystal Lodge.

"A number of merchants volunteered to be on the Board, they've just been waiting for the opportunity to get involved. The women are caring for the kids. And more good news, Johnny; I've ordered the rig dismantled from the Cripple River. We're gonna make Juneau a livable city, for you, me and the kids."

Johnny loved this woman more than he'd ever loved anyone. She was doing everything he'd always wanted to do. He didn't have to tell her; somehow she knew what had to be done. When Juneau was rid of the terror and corruption of Soapy Smith and his gang, a man could make a home for his wife and kids.

Johnny returned to the Hall for further instruction in Kali. Tony trained them in disarming a knife-wielding outlaw. He had them use a small stick in one hand and a Kali stick in the other.

"Should you find yourself against a knife-wielding man you must use the opposite hand to block the thrust, the reason being if you were to use the hand nearest you, you could effectively block the thrust but a slash would follow. By using the opposite hand you have kept your body away from a slash that would follow a block. Now I will teach you a wrist lock that would force your opponent to drop his knife, then you can follow up with a disabling blow.

I would prefer to have a Kali stick with me than a knife. You have a greater advantage over a knife wielder. These things I teach you can be shared with your family.

The martial arts are designed to protect life and foster peace. To insure the peace, training in the art of war is essential."

Just then the door to the Hall flew open. A man started yelling incoherently. "They've kidnapped my wife and three children. Look what you've started! Soapy Smith threatens to kill them unless we release his men and hand over his money. My wife was returning home from Pine Log when a dozen men blew up the train and killed the conductor and several passengers! They are holding ten people hostage. We must do as they say or he will kill all the hostages," said the hysterical man.

"What's your name mister, get a grip or, yourself," said Johnny as he tried to calm the man.

"Jeff Baxter, I have a claim north of here and a small farm. My wife and kids work it during the summer months. Now they're gone. He's going kill them; swore he would if we don't pay up."

"Do you know where Soapy and his men are, right now?" asked Dave.

"They camped at the base of Brood Mountain, about ten miles from here."

"O.K., tell Soapy he can bring his men in on Friday at noon. Tell him we'll have all the money we collected ready for him at the Town Meeting Hall, can you do that, Jeff? Tell him we'll be unarmed, so keep his men cool. He's to bring the hostages with him. Today is Wednesday; the money will be ready for him at noon on Friday. If any of the hostages are harmed, the deal is off. Tell him just what I said, Jeff. Now go!"

Dave gathered the men together. "Things are moving at a fast pace now. Johnny, I want the chairs at the Hall replaced with cane-backed chairs. Can you get that done for me?"

"Yea, we have some at Sue's place and others in storage."

"Tony, you'll loosen the backs so we can use them as weapons when we need them. When they come into town they will be ready to kill with firearms. We've got to lure them into complacency and lure them into a situation that we'll be at our best advantage. Then we'll strike hard. It'll be dangerous, so there's still time to back out if any of you men feel the odds are against us. They are numerically superior, but with cunning and training we can beat them. I can't impress on you the importance of what you have learned in the martial arts, but I can tell you a true story. My friend, Funokoshi was a conscript in the Japanese army. During physical training the men in his barracks derided his knowledge of Karate and decided to put him to the test. Eighty men surrounded him. They were six deep in a mob circle. The ringleader gave the order to attack and pummel him. At the first charge, Funokoshi leaped into the air. When the group retreated to survey their damage, six men were lying on the ground moaning in great pain. The ringleader ordered another attack. Again, six more were injured. The ground was littered with wounded men. The attackers could not believe their eyes. One man against eighty; now twelve were injured. The ringleader called an attack for the third time. This time the men ran away.

"I tell you this story because we will have to strike so fast as to demoralize their spirit in the first minute of combat. The training you have received will make all the difference. Now here is the plan..." The men listened intently to Dave as he outlined exactly what he wanted each man to do.

"Johnny, have the bank bring us the money, plus bags of gold nuggets. Tell them we guarantee they'll be returned. Only seven of us will be in the Hall when the exchange takes place. We must lull them into thinking we are compliant and fearful. Each man will be low-key and subservient and maneuver into position among

Soapy's men in order to take out two to three men in less than a minute. We must minimize the chance that guns will be fired. Kyoto and I will target the most aggressive of their leaders and stay near them. Johnny, you will have to take out Soapy. We will try to draw most of their men around a large table where the cane back chairs and piles of money and nuggets will be.

"Several large, heavy, empty chests will be in the back of the room. They will have to retrieve them. The moment I open the chest, we strike like lightening. I will not open the chest unless I feel everyone is in position. Do you all understand that? In less than a minute I expect the battle to be over. All your training and reflexes have been sharpened for this minute in time. Now go home, get a good night's sleep and do not talk to anyone until we gather outside Town Hall at 11 a.m. No man is to be armed. Do you all understand? If you do as I say, you will see your families again and you will feel like a man."

# CHAPTER XX

The morning sun cast a series of shadowed stripes across the cot and woke Johnny from his restless sleep. He cast off the blankets and looked around him at the prison cell. Sparse accommodations Juneau offered, just as well you don't want them thinking it's a hotel. He stayed the night in the cell not wanting to tell Sue about today's meeting with Soapy and his men. She'd worry too much. Just then the front door opened. Tony walked in tentatively followed by a smiling black man whose muscles rippled under a deerskin jacket.

"Johnny, I want you to meet T. K. Buracca. He would like to help us out today. He is a master at Kali. I knew him in San Francisco when he lived with a Filipino family and learned the art from a master."

Johnny shook hands with T. K. and felt he was a good omen. "Not many people would want to volunteer for what we have to do; you thought about it?"

"Tony is like family; my friends in Frisco would like to see him again. When he told me what you all plan to do, I figured you could use some help."

"Glad to have you aboard T. K. Here's what we plan to do; see how you fit in," Johnny outlined Dave's plan. "Soapy and his men will be in town in three hours. They have a number of hostages, I think I'd like you to remain with the hostages and subdue those holding them," said Johnny, "We'll be inside Town Hall with Soapy and his men negotiating their release. When we strike you'll be on your own resources, until we get out of there."

"I'll pretend to be a stable hand, Johnny; this way I can get close to them."

"They'll be armed and dangerous; some are killers, T. K."

"I hear ya."

Johnny walked over to Town Hall to check on the arrangements. Mr. Tully, the banker was reluctant to part with so much cash and gold bullion, but finally agreed to "lend" what he could because of the hostage situation. Several men were outside the Hall unloading the empty chests from a covered wagon. Once inside, Johnny had a workman place cast iron ballast's on the bottom to weigh down the boxes.

The cane-backed chairs were brought in, placed around the table and scattered about the Hall. Johnny walked over to one, lifted the headpiece off the chair and pulled out a stick two feet in length. He whipped it into an *X* cut and continued the form Tony had taught: parry, block, cut, trap and release, strike. He repeated the form then set the cane back into the chair. Mr. Tully, the banker came in with several clerks carrying sacks of gold nuggets and cash.

"There you are Brady, over $100,000 of the bank's assets. You don't stand a snowball's chance in hell of keeping Soapy from grabbing the loot. He'll probably kill you all in the process. And you'll be taking the bank down with you. I'm holding you alone responsible for this mess. The townspeople will be up in arms when they hear of our losses. Where are your men? I was expecting to see an army hiding in ambush but there's hardly a soul in the street."

"Don't worry about my men; they'll be here when needed. What time is it?"

"Eleven a.m", said Tully as he glanced at his gold pocket watch.

"You'll have your money back in two hours," said Johnny as he glanced around the room. Everything was ready. He followed Mr. Tully outside and locked the Hall behind him.

He looked up at the church tower across the street from Town Hall. A man in the bell tower was signaling in an agitated manner. They were coming! How many? The man in the tower went back to his binoculars. He seemed to look for a time. How many, dammit?

The man in the tower finally motioned with quick downward thrusts of his arm. Johnny counted: *one, two, three, four, five, six, seven, eight, nine, ten, eleven, twelve, thirteen, fourteen, fifteen, sixteen, seventeen, eighteen, nineteen, twenty, twenty-one, twenty-two, twenty-three, twenty-four...* Oh come on, that's enough, thought Johnny. *Twenty-five, twenty-six, twenty-seven, twenty-eight, twenty-nine, thirty, thirty-one...* Dave was at his side now. *Thirty-two, thirty-three, thirty-four, thirty-five, thirty-six, thirty-seven,* and then he finally stopped motioning.

He's got thirty-seven men riding with him, Dave."

"It's going to be interesting, Johnny, but remember my friend, Funokoshi; he had eighty men against him."

"That may be so, Dave, but they weren't carrying Colt .45's and Winchester rifles."

"Well, that's the part that's interesting, Johnny. Did you ever hear of mind boxing? It's using the powers of the mind to outbox and outfox your opponent. You can disarm men with the powers of the mind, Johnny. I'll help you. When Soapy gets here, introduce me as Mr. David, the city treasurer."

Johnny could now hear the faint din of many men on horseback coming from the north end of town. The speck grew larger and larger. He could now make out an outboard wagon trailing behind them. Johnny looked around and he could see Big Jack Schwartz standing at the door to his store. Kyoto was ambling down the sidewalk. He had his chef uniform on. There was Willie tending to a horse. Huang was peering out of a window of his shop. Tony and T. K. were unloading a wagon nearby. The thunder of hooves was growing louder. People were starting to run for cover from the horde of riders galloping at full speed down Main Street. Soapy was in the lead wearing a long leather overcoat and a full beard. The trail of men and wagons slowed to a trot as they approached the two lone figures standing in the middle of the town square. Steam emanated from the nostrils of the heated horses as Soapy reared back on the reins and brought the hostile group of men and wagons to a halt. Some of the men drew their pistols while others withdrew carbines from saddle holsters.

"Soapy, you can tell your men to put away their guns. We're completely unarmed, we want a peaceful exchange," said Johnny.

Soapy turned in the saddle and checked the rooftops and shops for snipers. The few men visible had stopped doing their chores and were now watching the encounter in the town square. "I'll be giving the orders around here, sheriff. Where's those taxes you people owe?"

"Where's the Baxter clan, Soapy? There'll be no exchange unless they're released."

"They're resting in the rear wagon, now where's the taxes?"

"Dave, go take a look and see if they're O. K."

Dave walked a hundred feet to the last wagon and pulled away a tarpaulin. Underneath, squirming against tight, rope restraints were the Baxter's and six other hostages. Dave reassured them everything was going to be O. K. and walked to Johnny's side. "They're tied up, but they appear to be O.K.," said Dave appearing frightened and meek.

"Why'd you kill those people on the train, Soapy?"

"Cause they got in my way, and I'll plug you too if things don't go to my liking," said Soapy as he withdrew the biggest pistol Johnny had ever seen.

"Mr. Smith, sir," interjected Dave. "There ain't no need to be violent. I'm sure you will find everything to your liking, sir. We've arranged for a peaceful exchange, sir."

"And who might you be, you little runt?"

"I'm Mr. Fresney, the city treasurer, Mr. Brady asked me to make all the arrangements for the orderly transfer of those "taxes" you requested. I have an aversion to firearms, Mr. Smith. Do you think you and your men could restrain themselves? This could be the first of many... uh, "tax -collecting arrangements," and I'd like them to go smoothly if you don't mind, Mr. Smith?"

Soapy looked around again, "O.K. men, take it easy. Put away the guns. We don't want to ruin those "tax collecting procedures" that'll be taking place frequently. Right, Mr. Fresney?"

"At your convenience, sir," said Dave with a toothy smile.

"Now, let's get down to business. Where's the cash and nuggets you collected for us, Brady?"

"First, free the hostages and you'll get your money," said Johnny.

"Mr. Brady, you don't seem to understand," Soapy drew his large gun again and pointed it at Johnny, "I give the orders around here. They'll be freed when I say so."

Dave pleaded, "I'm sure Mr. Brady will accept your conditions. Won't you, sheriff?"

"You're right, Mr. Fresney. We want this to go smoothly. I guess you'll want to inspect the cash and gold nuggets. They're stored in the Town Hall. I hope you don't mind, but a few of the town citizens might want to witness the exchange. Since it's going to be on a frequent basis, we might as well let them in on it. Wouldn't want them to think the city treasurer has absconded with their savings," said Johnny as he looked on Dave's blushing countenance. "You men come here," yelled Johnny. "We need you to witness a peaceful exchange for the Baxter clan!"

"Yea, we want to involve the citizens in *the tax collecting procedures*, don't we boys?" guffawed Soapy, laughing so much he had to wipe the spittle from the corners of his mouth. "Tax collecting procedures," he chortled as five unarmed citizens meekly approached the violent men.

# CHAPTER XXI

The large crowd of men entered through the oak doors of Town Hall. At the far end of the Hall there was a table loaded down with bags of gold nuggets and piles of cash. Soapy's men whistled with delight at the prospect of a payday. Johnny, Dave, Soapy Smith, and three of his henchmen went around to the front of the table. Soapy ordered the rest of his men away from the table. "There'll be plenty for you all to gawk at when we get this cache to Brood Mountain. How much do you reckon is here, sheriff?"

"Over two hundred thousand in cash and gold, Mr. Smith," interjected Dave.

Soapy opened a few bags and pulled out a nugget from each. He bit into each nugget and held it up to the light. "It's real enough," he said as he fondled the nuggets. "You done a good job, sheriff; keeping up your end of the bargain." He beamed, "You too, Mr. Treasurer." Dave smiled brightly back. Soapy's men relaxed and smiled at the witnesses.

"Then you'll release the Baxter clan, Soapy?" asked Johnny.

"Whoa there, sheriff! Hold your horses! Let's complete this transaction before we start making demands. You ain't exactly in the position to be making demands now, are you? Is he men?" Soapy leered at his men as they responded in unison.

"No way, Soapy!" A few of the men raised their firearms to emphasize the point. The witnesses to the transaction reacted with fear and trembling. Slowly the men holstered their guns and lowered their rifles, smiling at their dominance of the situation.

"You men over there, bring those trunks up here so we can load this stuff!" barked Soapy.

The two trunks were brought up to the table. Soapy attempted to open them but they were locked.

"Oh, Mr. Smith, let me open them. I have the keys right here," said Dave as he fumbled for the keys he had in his pocket. He inserted the key into the trunk and smiled as he glanced down at the assembled crowd. He waited.

"Well go ahead and open it! What are you waiting for?" barked Soapy.

"I seem to have trouble getting the key into the right position."

There was movement in the crowd below. Soapy's men grew impatient, then relaxed as Dave said, "there I got it."

He jerked open the trunk and the Hall exploded in pandemonium. Dave had positioned himself to be near the three men with Soapy. His hand had left the trunk in an instant. He was a fighting machine. In five seconds all three men were disabled and in varying degrees of pain. One reached for his gun, while on the floor, but a series of kicks and multiple blows rendered him unconscious.

A shot rang out. Dave turned to see two men who had managed to escape from the melee and were trying to target a victim from the whirling bodies around them. He leaped on the table and, in an instant, was flying through the air. Two well-placed kicks in the faces of both men temporarily blinded them, but they managed to hold onto their guns firing wildly. A series of instant blows and hand locks disarmed them as they lay sprawled on the floor.

Dave pulled two fighting sticks from a chair and entered the fray. Willie Annue was being pummeled by a huge man who was positioning the butt end of a rifle for a crashing blow. Dave hooked and parried the rifle with one stick and delivered two stinging whacks which caused the man to release his grip on the rifle. In an instant Dave delivered multiple blows and the man was writhing in pain. Huge red welts covered his face. Dave turned from him and assessed the situation. His assessment took half a second and he rejoined the pandemonium.

Kyoto was leaping in the air, delivering well placed Karate kicks to a number of combatants. The floor was now littered with men who were battered and bruised and in varying degrees of pain. The fight was going out of many of them and some scampered to the safety of the wall, throwing up their arms in surrender. Others however, were now using chairs and were flinging them at Johnny's men.

Tony was using his sticks in a methodical way. Deflecting some thrown furniture with one, delivering rapid blows in a rhythmic motion almost resembling a dance. Another shot was fired and, in an instant, the gun clattered to the floor as one of Soapy's men held his wrist in agony from the stick blow to his shooting arm. A thrust to his abdomen made him double-up in pain, while a blow to his neck sent him sprawling to the floor.

Chuck Harris picked up one of Soapy's men and targeted a group of men who were about to charge Sergeant Fenwick as he disabled an assailant with one blow. Chuck flung the man through the air; his body landed squarely on the backs of three men. The force of the throw rocketed them to the floor. "Thanks, Chuck!" yelled Fenwick as he dragged the men to the wall.

Twenty seconds had elapsed. Curses and screams were beginning to lessen in intensity. Johnny's men sensed victory as their bodies reacted in trained discipline moves to the onslaught of blows coming their way. The targets were becoming more individualized as fewer men were involved in the fighting. Sergeant Fenwick was even in the process of picking up weapons from the floor as Chuck fought with three men in front of him.

In front of the table a battle of titans was taking place. Johnny had disabled Soapy with three quick blows, but was jumped from behind by two of Soapy's men as he tried to remove the guns from Soapy's waistband. He fought off the assailants with parries and blocks, then a rapid series of blows. In the interim, Soapy had got to his feet and tried to retrieve his guns, which had been thrown against a wall, but the melee prevented him from reaching them. He grabbed Johnny in a stranglehold. Johnny reversed a kick to his scrotum and shot back with two elbows deep into his ribs. Soapy howled with pain and released his grip. Johnny spun around and dealt a series of palm strikes to Soapy's chin, grabbed his arm and sent him sprawling to the floor. Soapy didn't move. Johnny went over to the trunks on the table and took lengths of rope and bound his arms and legs. He left Soapy and rejoined his friends as they finished off the remaining combatants.

With the battle over, Johnny and his men bound the wrists of Soapy's men and led them toward the judge's chambers, which had a solid oak door and grated windows. It would act as a temporary holding pen until they could be brought to the jail. Johnny, Dave, Tony, Kyoto, Willie Annue, Sergeant Fenwick and Chuck smiled in triumph at what they had accomplished. They cleaned their wounds and talked animatedly about the battle.

Town citizens volunteered to act as jailers and, one by one, Soapy and his men were led away. T. K. Barracca and Big Jack Schwartz joined Johnny inside the Hall. "We had very little problem taking care of the men on horseback, a few well-placed whacks and they were unseated and subdued," said T. K.

"The Baxter clan is fine, they're a family again," smiled Big Jack Schwartz.

The men left the Hall in groups. Johnny asked Dave what he planned to do now that his work was over.

"I'm going back to England to rejoin my students and to teach," said Dave, completely unscathed from the fierce battle. "What are you and Sue going to do, Johnny?"

"I'm going to get married, Dave, and start a family right away. Juneau will be a lot safer now."

"It's about time!" said Dave with a boyish grin.

John (James) Green Brady (May 25, 1847–December 17, 1918) was an American politician who was the governor of the district of Alaska from 1897 to 1906. He arrived in New York City on a coffin ship during the Irish Potato Famine (1845-1852). He was orphaned at an early age and was found living in a sewer pipe by Theodore Roosevelt Sr., a well-known and popular New York City philanthropist and father of the future U.S. president, Theodore Roosevelt. Many years later, as an adult, Brady approached the younger Theodore Roosevelt, (then the governor of New York) in 1900, at a conference in Portland, Oregon, warmly shook his hand and told him the following story:

"Governor Roosevelt, the other governors have greeted you with interest, simply as a fellow governor and a great American, but I greet you with infinitely more interest, as the son of your father, the first Theodore Roosevelt" when greeted warmly by Governor Roosevelt and asked why and in what special way he had been interested in his father, Governor Brady replied, "Your father picked me up on the streets of New York, a waif and an orphan, and sent me to a western family, paying for my early care and transportation. Years passed and I was able to repay the money, but I can never repay what he did for me, for it was through that early care and by giving me such a foster mother and father that I gradually rose in the world until I greet his son as a fellow governor of a part of our great country."

After being picked up from the orphan train, he lived with the family of John Green of Tipton County, Indiana. He married Elizabeth Jane Patton in 1887 in Sitka, Alaska. He had children: John Green Brady Jr., Hugh P. Brady, Sheldon Jackson, Mary Anna Brady and Elizabeth P. Brady. He attended Yale University and graduated in 1874.

Brady moved to the Alaska Territory, first as a Presbyterian minister, missionary and lawyer. He co-founded what is now Sheldon Jackson College as a school for training Alaska natives in 1878. Later he would be appointed governor for three terms. He was introduced to the infamous Alaskan bad man, Soapy Smith during the July 4th, 1898 festivities in Skagway. Brady was made aware of Soapy's criminal activities and offered him a position as a deputy U.S. marshal in Sitka if he would quit Skagway. Soapy turned down the position and Brady noted it in a personal letter. Four days after meeting him, Soapy was killed in the famed shootout on Juneau wharf.

Brady died on December 17, 1918 and was buried in Sitka National Cemetery. The monument bears the inscription: "a life ruled by faith in god and man."

46659212R00067

Made in the USA
Charleston, SC
22 September 2015